SOLARA

ZOE KARIBIAN

MAPLE
PUBLISHERS

Author: Zoe Karibian

First Published in 2025

ISBN 978-1-83538-840-2 (Paperback)
       978-1-83538-841-9 (Hardback)
       978-1-83538-842-6 (E-Book)

Book Layout by:
       Maple Publishers
       www.maplepublishers.com

Book Cover design and Artwork by:
       Aram Karakachian

Published by:
       Maple Publishers
       Fairbourne Drive, Atterbury,
       Milton Keynes,
       MK10 9RG, UK
       www.maplepublishers.com

To my brother, Leo, and sister,
Maya—who may (or may not)
have inspired a character or two.

The proceeds from the sale of this book in its first
year are gifted to the Shamida Orphanage in Ethiopia.

A very special thanks to my talented friend
Aram Karakachian for designing the cover.

CONTENTS

1. The Healer 5

2. The Home 11

3. The Mentor 16

4. The Conversation 23

5. The Trio 32

6. The Visit 43

7. The Light 54

8. The Prince 60

9. The Message 67

10. The Second Visit 72

11. The Father 78

12. The Voice 85

13. The Aquara 92

14. The Meeting 97

15. The Rebels 107

16. The Sickness 115

17. The Emberberry 126

18. The Protectors 129

19. The Father 134

20. The King 139

21. The Final Breath 145

22. The Bombing 151

23. The Fire 159

24. The Aftermath 169

25. The Council 183

26. The Desert..186

27. The Water...193

28. The Throne 202

About The Author..209

1

The Healer

Between the dead patient, the drunk men and the Blood Sun, my day was not off to a fantastic start.

Streams of intoxicated people stumbled through Sand City's dusty alleys, their catcalls and slurred sentences an unwelcome refrain on my walk home. The city center pulsed ahead, a dense knot of life and noise. Narrow passageways, just wide enough for me to brush both walls with my fingertips, spilled into wider streets baked by the relentless sun. Buildings pressed close together, two or three stories high, their mud-brick walls cracked and sun-bleached to the color of bone. Faded paint clung in stubborn patches. Wooden shutters sagged on rusted hinges. Above, crooked balconies leaned into the street, patched with scrap wood and warped metal, laundry lines sagging between them like drooping ropes

Sand City's market bled into every available space. Rickety stalls leaned against the buildings, their canopies stitched from colorful cloth. Each stall overflowed with mismatched goods–dried herbs stacked in wicker baskets, scraps of old machinery piled in precarious towers, trinkets of glass, bone and colored wire whose uses were anyone's guess. Vendors hawked their prices, desperate to catch the attention of customers before the heat drove them away. The air was thick with dust, sweat and sharp herbs, a jumble of scents that tangled in your nose and refused to let go.

The street itself was a jigsaw of bodies. People jostled past, elbows grazing ribs, feet scraping against loose stones that sent little clouds of ochre dust swirling into the air. Some staggered drunkenly, eyes glazed, while others moved with urgent precision: heads low, fingers clenched around parcels or small leather pouches that clinked faintly with coins.

Each step kicked up a fresh cloud of dust that clung to my skin, my clothes, and burned in my lungs. By this hour, the heat pressed down like a smothering hand. My cheeks stung, pink and tender beneath the blazing sun, while wisps of brown hair worked loose from my braid and plastered themselves against my flushed face.

My full-length tunic, a muted linen garment passed down from my mother, darkened with sweat. I had pulled a shawl low over my face. It was a flimsy barrier against the swirling grit and, more importantly, against prying eyes. Though I steered clear of roaming hands, I could not avoid the hooded eyes that followed me with a little too much interest.

The Blood Sun was not helping. At dawn, a thick haze had settled across the sky, bathing Sand City in an eerie scarlet glow. As the sun rose to its midday peak, it seemed to make the early summer heat scorch hotter, thicker, *angrier*.

"I hate days like this," Naila muttered.

I looked over to my tan-skinned cousin beside me. Her honey-brown eyes turned skyward, the corners of her lips hooking into a frown. Strands of dark hair gleamed on her head while the freckles speckled on her cheeks seemed more defined than ever. Her beige tunic was perfectly folded around her shoulders and her hair was impeccably groomed into a low bun.

Naila was only two years older than me, but she carried herself like someone who had lived twice as long. We had been apprentices at the healers' center for almost a year now, and while I sometimes struggled to keep up with the relentless demands, Naila thrived on the order of it all. She had a way of making decisions swiftly. It was no surprise that the healers often trusted her with more complicated tasks.

Today, though, even she seemed frayed.

"Solis Day is bad enough without this infernal heat," she said.

I hummed in agreement. Rising temperatures brought rising tempers, and that meant more fights, more injuries, and more patients.

"The healers' center will be a madhouse this evening," I added. "I can come back with you, if you'd like. I'm sure the apprentices would appreciate some extra hands."

"Your mother and I can handle things for the rest of the day. Go on home and rest, you had a rough morning shift."

I flinched at the memory.

Naila set her smooth hand on my forearm and gave it a squeeze. "It was not your fault, Solara."

"I know," I lied.

A patient died on my watch today. He had been far younger than his weathered features implied, orphaned and swallowed up by the slums of Sand City. On the brink of starvation, he had tried to snatch rations from a vendor's cart and received a knife between the ribs in return. By the time I arrived, he had lost too much blood, his breath raspy and wet from a collapsed lung.

I could do nothing but hold his hand and murmur the sacred prayer of Eternal Rest. The life dimmed from his green eyes while the bustle of the marketplace continued around us, uninterrupted. "Strange to have a Blood Sun on Solis Day this year," I said, eager to change the subject.

I tucked a wisp of brown hair behind my ear, its hue complemented by the olive tone of my sun-drenched skin. My focus rose to the crimson orb glaring down at us. "Feels like a bad omen."

In the old times, a Blood Sun was said to be a warning from the Gods, a harbinger of great upheaval. An appearance generations ago on the eve of civil war, a conflict we now call The Great Divide in its honor, had reinforced its ominous reputation. Its recurrence now, on Solis Day no less, was sure to ignite speculation.

"Nonsense," Naila said with a dismissive swish of her hand. "A silly superstition, nothing more. We had one two decades ago and no harm came of it."

"My darling little brother might disagree with you," I said. "That Blood Sun was the day of my birth."

Her eyebrows rose. "Was it really?"

I nodded. "He has fun reminding me whenever the Blood Sun is due."

I smiled at the memory. *Even the Gods knew you'd be a pain in the ass,* Kian would say with a grin, before fleeing out of my reach.

I smiled at the memory, though a growing unease clouded my thoughts. Even Naila could not hide the deep crease in her brow as she followed my gaze to the sky.

"Are you and Tarek going to do anything to celebrate?" she asked.

A flush rose to my cheeks. Tarek was my oldest and dearest friend but, lately, "friend" felt too small a word for the way we held hands or kissed each other goodnight.

"He refuses to celebrate Solis Day on principle," I said, sighing. "He says it's the most depressing day of the year."

"It's rare a young man turns down the chance to drown himself in free wine and run around the city with no consequences."

"Believe me, Naila, if the wine were from Haren, Tarek would be the first to take full advantage. He would be dancing through the streets of Sand City, stumbling through alleys, rolling around in the bushes—" Naila snorted softly.

"He objects to Aquara wine?"

"He objects to the Aquara."

"At least that explains why he finds Solis Day depressing."

"Yep."

Though Solis Day was our most raucous holiday, it was not one that people of Sand City looked on with fondness. On this day many millennia ago, four leaders known as The Elders carved our world, Aetherium, into four regions. The partition came in the wake of Earth's environmental collapse after industrial waste contaminated the planet's water and soil. Rivers, lakes, and oceans were poisoned with mercury and other toxins, making the water undrinkable and the land nearly impossible to farm. Only a few crops, like potatoes and root vegetables, could survive in the polluted soil, but even those became harder to grow as the land's fertility decreased.

The Elders created the four regions to manage the limited resources left. Haren became the center for salvaged technology and relics, while Terra took control of the last agricultural land. Ignios was dedicated to military training and Aquara was in charge of healing.

By creating the regions, The Elders hoped to usher in an era of peace and prosperity where the regions could coexist, but their vision was never fully realized. The regions were unevenly distributed and, while most were left in desolation, Aquara prospered. It had access to the last remaining clean water, stored in deep underground reservoirs untouched by contamination. While the other regions fought over dwindling resources, Aquara held a monopoly on water and the means to purify it.

Solis Day was meant to remind us of that collective, lofty goal. However, to most of us in the region of Haren, it was just a reminder of how far reality had fallen short of that dream.

"I wonder what the Aquara do to celebrate Solis," I mused, gazing out beyond the rooftops. Far in the distance, I could just make out the faint, shimmering outline of the Royal Palace's imposing spires.

"My cousin works in one of the grand homes there and she says it's a thing to behold. Daytime spent twirling streamers and nibbling fruit in the wildflower fields, evening spent dancing in gowns and jewels. Buffets as far as the eye can see and musicians playing from dusk to dawn."

"Sounds about right," I hummed. "It is their day after all."

The day that control of Aetherium's resources passed to them by way of inheritance, one of many gifts bestowed upon them by The Elders. Haren was not granted such generosity.

"It's shameful, if you ask me," Naila huffed. "Today is meant to be about the Aquara and the other realms coming together, yet they go out of their way to shut us out."

"Who would have thought," I deadpanned. "They're normally so kind and welcoming."

For all my sarcasm, I had never actually met an Aquara myself. Despite growing up a short walk from Nereidia, the wealthy capital of their region and home to the elite ruling class, I might as well have lived a world away. As a child, my mother had established a few ground rules: No consuming their food or wine. No venturing into Nereidia. I was not even permitted to treat Aquara patients in my work as a healer.

The only contact she could not protect me from was the occasional brush with the cold-hearted soldiers of the Royal Guard who patrolled the border between Sand City and Nereidia. Today, even they were noticeably absent. Having placated us with morning shipments of free wine, the King had pulled his guards and left us to our own devices for the day.

As Naila and I pressed through the bustling streets, we eventually stopped by Haren's healing center, a white-washed concrete cube nestled between two other unassuming structures. The entrance was marked by two swinging glass doors, adorned with a carved emblem of intertwined leaves and water droplets, an ancient symbol of healing and life. The cool air hit our faces as we stepped in, carrying with it the faint scent of medicinal herbs.

The familiar hum of activity greeted us. Healers moved with purpose, tending to patients with gentle hands and focused expressions. Shelves lined the walls, stocked with an array of dried herbs, vials of potions and various healing implements. It was here that my mother had spent countless hours refining the art of healing and passing down the knowledge that had been in our family for generations.

Naila, always observant, noticed the weariness in my eyes and placed a comforting hand on my shoulder. "Rest, Solara," she said softly, her voice as smooth as polished glass. "You've been pushing yourself too hard. Go home."

I could never tell if Naila's serene demeanor was born of genuine care or condescension, but I nodded anyway, "Alright," I said. "See you later."

I cast one last look around the healers' center before stepping through the sliding glass doors and onto the street.

2

The Home

After winding through the narrow alleys that led out of Sand City's center, our little hut finally came into view. It was a simple little home tucked away in the quieter parts of Haren that meandered west from the border of Aquara. My father had built it entirely from scratch using sun-bleached timbers and earthy clay.

This house had always been my safe harbor, filled with memories of sitting on the front porch creating tinctures with my mother, sparring with my father and chasing my brother, Kian, through the spiraling streets that wreathed the home like a protective shield.

A single, weathered wooden door creaked as it swung open, its hinges straining from years of use. The interior was lit by rays of sunlight that pierced through gaps in the walls and roof, casting fleeting patterns on the floor. Our house contained just the essentials: a rickety wooden table, a couple of mismatched chairs and a few mattresses for sleeping. In the corner a soot-stained fireplace sat unused, waiting for the cold nights when Mother, Father, Kian and I would huddle around its flickering flame.

"I'm back," I called breathily. No answer.

A wooden cabinet at the entrance displayed a small assortment of trinkets and faded photographs. Maps that were parched with age adorned the walls, bearing scrawled notes and routes that navigated the region of Haren.

I had always been fascinated by maps. The intricate lines and symbols held a promise of discovery. I often found myself lost in their labyrinthine details. My aunt, who had worked as a Relic—a guardian and scholar of Haren's deep underground libraries, tasked with preserving the ancient texts left by past generations—had fueled this passion by gifting me a map on my seventh birthday. It was a hand-drawn piece with delicate ink strokes and I spent hours studying it, imagining the bustling workshops of the Technology District, the narrow market streets of Sand City and even the hidden paths that led to forgotten ruins beyond the city's borders.

Pulling my gaze away from the maps, my eyes fell upon my younger brother, Kian, who was hunched over our small wooden desk cluttered with an assortment of objects he had collected from scavenging.

"Hey," I called out with a weary smile, approaching the desk.

"Oh, you're back!" he replied, pushing back a few unruly locks of his sandy hair. The blond strands stood out against his sun-kissed skin, a trait passed down from generations of Haren citizens.

"Yeah, made it back in one piece," I replied, wiping some dust from my cheek and sinking into a nearby chair.

"What's this?"

Kian's face broke into an impish grin, revealing a smudge of dirt on his cheek. "My Hovercar was missing some brakes," he said, gesturing towards the pile of salvaged parts. "Made a stop by the scrapyard on the way home."

The scrapyard was one of Kian's favorite places. As kids, we would go there after school and make makeshift forts and castles out of the discarded metal and wood. We would spend hours pretending to be kings and queens of our little domains, imagining grand adventures amidst the rusted remains of old machinery.

Even now, Kian's eyes sparkled with that same childlike excitement whenever he talked about his finds. "You should have seen the stuff I found today," he said, using animated hand gestures to add color to his words. "There was this old motor from a fan, some copper tubing and even a few gears that looked almost new. I think I can use them to get the Hovercar running again."

I rolled my eyes, a smirk playing on my lips. "You and your junkyard treasures. You always think you've struck gold." Leaning back in my chair, I added, "Remember the time we found that old radio? We spent weeks trying to get it to work."

Kian laughed, the sound bright and infectious. "Yeah, and we ended up just using it as a storage box for our other treasures." He glanced at the desk, now cluttered with his latest haul. "Guess not much has changed."

He picked up the bundle of wires and metal again, his fingers deftly twisting them into place. "Anyway, this brake system should be good as new once I'm done with it. Just need to tweak a few more things."

I tilted my head to the side, skeptical. "*That's* a brake? I swear, Kian, sometimes I think you're just messing with me."

His fingers danced over the wires, bending and twirling them with precision until they formed a mechanism. "Oh, have a little faith," he teased in Father's voice, flashing me a playful smile.

With a satisfied grin, Kian reached for a peculiar object, handling it with the utmost care. It was a small, boxy device with a circular dial on its face, surrounded by numbers and an array of strange, round buttons. According to Kian's shaky knowledge of artifacts, he believed it was one of those objects described in the Haren manuscripts used millennia ago to talk to someone at a distance. I could not even picture it. All the people I could ever care to talk to were right around me.

The object's black plastic casing was worn but intact as Kian dismantled it with expert ease, reverently laying each part on the workbench as if they were precious gems. He carefully extracted the copper wiring, the tiny gears and the speaker cone, integrating them into his design.

His hunched back and blackened fingers reminded me sharply of our father. Kian spent long hours in the Technology District, crouched on a small stool in sweltering buildings. He liked to joke about his work, often reciting the district's slogan: "The place where ingenuity thrives!" Yet, the cuts on his fingers and the exhaustion in his eyes betrayed him.

The factories in the Technology District of Haren were no gentle thing. Outside, they appeared as a sprawling complex of corrugated iron and steel. Inside, the environment was a cacophony of clanging metal, hissing steam and the low hum of machinery. I had visited those factories once and seen firsthand the grime and grit of relentless labor. Conveyor belts snaked through the factory floor, carrying half-assembled devices past rows of workers who added components with precise movements. The heat was oppressive, amplified by the machinery and the lack of ventilation.

As much as the smell of disinfectant and the sight of elderly people in beds could make bile rise in my throat, I would pick it any day over the Technology District. At least in the healers' center there was an air of calm and purpose, a sense of doing good. I reminded myself that this was what Kian loved. It was his choice, his passion, but I could not help but worry about the toll it was taking on him.

Besides, some people truly had it worse. My aunt had once told me about the crop tenders in Terra: Aetherium's region dedicated entirely to agriculture. Unlike Haren, where one could choose between the pursuit of knowledge in Relic, the innovation of machinery in Tech, or various side jobs like Healer or Guard, Terra offered no such diversity. Their lives revolved around the soil and the seasons. The crop tenders were forced to wake up at earliest hours, long before the first light of dawn. They spent their days under the scorching sun, bending over rows of crops. By the time they returned during the sun's late hours, their backs were on the brink of breaking and their fingers were dyed brown from hours of digging in the soil. It was some of the most grueling work imaginable. After all, the realm of Terra was designed to churn out produce and supply it to the rest of us. Without their relentless efforts, Aquara would never grant them the generous rations of water they received. The system ensured that Terra's people were perpetually bound to their fields.

As my eyes began to feel heavy, I told Kian goodnight and asked him to let Mother and Father know I was asleep when they returned home.

Kian and I shared a modest bedroom. Two mattresses lay a few feet apart on a floor covered with worn but clean blankets. The walls were bare except for a small shelf cluttered with a few cherished keepsakes and a stack of well-thumbed books. A single window, its shutters slightly askew, let in the cool night air and the soft hum of the city beyond.

I made my way to the adjacent washroom. The room featured a stone countertop carved with a basin and a nylon hose that protruded out of the wall, an inviting luxury on days when the hose chose to run water.

Above the basin hung a mirror, its surface coated in a light haze and a web of fine cracks that etched their way into a corner. Still, it did the job. I gazed at my reflection, tucking loose strands of hair behind my ears.

I twisted the little lever next to the hose and whispered a little prayer to the Sun Goddess but, to my disappointment, nothing but a single drop rolled out lazily from the hose. I groaned. No doubt the King had ordered Nereidia to shut off the water for Solis Day.

I headed back to my room and sank into my mattress, the distant laughter of revelers filtering in. I watched as the last of the day slid down the wall. Some light lingered after the sunset, pooling in the room, so that for a brief moment the piles of old clothes took on more shape and color than they had outside. I closed my eyes, letting the sounds and sights of home lull me to sleep.

3

The Mentor

There was an unusual sense of quiet in the house when I woke the next morning. Soft morning light filtered through the cracks in the shutters, casting a golden glow across the room. I slid out of bed, my feet making contact with the chalky limestone floor, and moved cautiously towards the main area where the faint aroma of herbs and spices guided me to the kitchen.

Naila was already by the table, her slender fingers tucking a few things away into her worn leather satchel. Rolls of bandages, jars of herbal salves and small bags filled with tinctures and ointments disappeared into the depths of the bag, each item placed with the precision of someone who knew their importance. Naila had been coming and going from our house since we were kids, moving with the easy familiarity of a sister, even if she was only my cousin.

"I let myself in. Didn't want to wake you up," she said.

"Heading out to the healers' center?"

"Yeah," she replied, turning to me with a soft smile. "It'll be pretty busy today with all the cases from the Solis Day festivities."

I did not need her to explain. After the festivities, men often arrived at the center in foul moods, bruised from tavern brawls, squabbling over stolen rations and still staggering from the celebrations.

Naila picked up her bags with a fluid grace and paused at the door, her eyes meeting mine. "I left some rations for you. Don't forget to eat… and, uh, tidy up the kitchen when you can," she said with a small smile before slipping out.

After Naila left, the house felt rather empty. It was always quiet, but today the silence felt heavier, broken only by the distant sounds of the market and the occasional creak of the house as it settled in the heat.

Kian had left early for his shift at the Technology District, leaving behind the lingering scent of herbs he used to mask the industrial grime. I assumed Father had gone on his usual errands. A neat, hurried note from my mother lay on the kitchen table: she had been called to the Royal Palace to tend to a visiting noble who had fallen ill and would return later in the afternoon.

Liora, as those close to her called my mother, was a well-regarded healer in Haren. She could draw out the venom of a sand viper without leaving a scar, staunch the slow rot of waterborne infections and treat rashes that devoured the skin overnight. The Royal Palace of Aquara summoned her repeatedly to care for the Royal Family. Today was one of those days.

I stretched and let the stillness of the empty house settle over me. Hunger gnawed at my stomach, so I made my way to the kitchen. On the counter, several packaged rectangles lay waiting, their brownish-yellow hue familiar and uninviting. Wrapped in crinkling plastic, they were compressed slabs of nutrient-rich paste.

With a sigh of resignation, I peeled away the wrapper and took a bite. The texture was gritty, almost chalky, and clung to my tongue like sand. It tasted like chewing on a mixture of sawdust and dried pulp, with a faint hint of something that might have once been sweet. This was food to keep me going, just as it had every other morning.

As I continued to chew, the rations began to expand in my mouth, becoming a dense mass that filled my stomach with surprising efficiency. It was not satisfying in the way a proper meal would be, but it staved off the hunger by settling into my gut like a solid weight. I swallowed, the lump sliding down my throat with difficulty, and took another bite.

My eyes wandered to the window as I ate, watching the streets of Haren slowly come to life. People bustled about, their figures casting long shadows in the morning light.

I decided I would make a detour to Rhea's house before heading to my shift. My healer's duties did not begin until the afternoon, and her home was not far. After all, I had not seen her in several days, and the thought of her warm chatter tugged at me. Maybe a visit would shake off the lingering drowsiness and give me a semblance of productivity.

I packed a few items into my shoulder bag and slung the weapons belt around my waist. My daggers' leather sheaths thumped softly against my legs as I secured them with a clink of the brass buckle. I doubted they would come to use, but you could never be too sure.

Stepping outside, the searing air filled my lungs, and the red-hot sand immediately began to bite into the soles of my sandals. The route to Rhea's house was etched into my memory. I navigated winding paths that twisted through the heart of the city, slipping between dusty streets that eventually led me to her home.

Rhea's small house was wedged between two large weather-beaten concrete tower blocks that had seen better days. Despite its hidden location, the house was unmistakable. Its white façade was spotless, undeterred by the city's decay. The doorway was flanked by wild bursts of flowers in an eccentric mismatch of pots. The air here carried the subtle fragrance of wildflowers and herbs wafting from the little garden in the back that Rhea somehow kept alive.

Rhea was well-known in the neighborhood as a herbalist and botanist, a woman with a knack for nurturing life in places where it seemed impossible. Her life before arriving at Haren was a mystery, pieced together only through hushed whispers and speculative gossip. However, it was her small incubator that truly captured the community's imagination.

This incubator was no ordinary object. It was an elegant glass sphere, its surface glinting with an otherworldly sheen. Within its crystalline confines, a single pea tendril thrived. The miraculous sphere was a gift from the Aquara as a token of gratitude for some unknown service many years ago. No one knew the details but, Rhea was not one to share secrets.

In Haren's unforgiving climate, where blistering heat and relentless sandstorms decimated any hint of vegetation and the acid-scarred soil was a death sentence for even the hardiest of plants, Rhea's incubator was nothing short of a miracle. The tendril inside drew both awe and envy from the community. There were times when desperate souls tried to steal it, hoping to sell it to the highest bidder in the markets. After a few heated confrontations ended by Rhea's fierce combat skills, it was clear the incubator would belong to her and her alone.

As a child, I could not help but press my face against the incubator's glass, captivated by the little lush world inside. It was slightly fogged from the humidity within, and the soil looked rich and dark, brimming with vitality. Rhea cared for that pea with a maternal tenderness. Despite our collective amazement and frequent compliments, she merely brushed off our admiration with a wave of her hand. "Oh, it's just a trinket," she would say, her voice dismissive. She claimed the incubator was nothing more than a frivolous gift from an Aquara noble: a gift whose purpose and motive remained a mystery. Still, that did not stop us from weaving our own stories about it, giving it a name—Verdant— and imagining how it had come to be in her possession.

Many in the neighborhood considered Rhea eccentric, if not outright crazy. They would often gossip about her wild stories and peculiar habits, like the way she would mutter to herself while gardening or wear mismatched robes that seemed out of place. Her stories about the Aquara, tales of their mysterious rituals and the legendary water-temples held me spellbound. She spoke of her years as a Royal Botanist in their land, painting a vivid picture of a realm so different from Haren that it felt like a dream.

I climbed the creaking steps of her porch and knocked lightly. Almost before my knuckles had left the wood, the door swung open. Rhea stood there, her sharp, twinkling eyes sizing me up with a familiar mischief. Her silver hair was pulled back in a loose bun. Stray wisps framed her face, which was creased with laugh lines rather than wrinkles. Her dress seemed to be made from a riot of colored scarves, each one fluttering with every movement. "Solara, dearie! Come in, come in," she sang, grabbing my hand and pulling me inside with surprising strength for her age.

"How've you been?" she asked once I was inside.

"Same as usual," I muttered with a small smile.

The air inside her home was cool and fragrant, heavy with the scent of herbs and damp earth. My gaze was immediately drawn, as always, to the incubator sitting on its pedestal near the window. The pea tendril inside seemed to glow faintly, its green more vivid than anything I had ever seen in the wild.

"Still enchanted by the plant, I see," Rhea said, a teasing lilt in her voice as she moved gracefully to her workbench, where a pot of something fragrant simmered.

"It's just… so alive," I whispered, unable to tear my gaze away.

Rhea chuckled softly and joined me by the incubator, lightly tapping the glass. "This little tendril has survived because it has what it needs: care, protection and the right environment."

"Do you ever wonder why they gave it to you?" I asked, my curiosity getting the better of me.

Rhea's sharp eyes flicked to mine, her expression unreadable, though a knowing glint danced in her gaze. "The Aquara have their reasons, just as we all do," she said, her voice calm but deliberate. "They guard their secrets well."

I sighed, exasperated by her cryptic answer, but her lips curved into that sly smile I knew so well. Shifting the topic, I brushed a thin layer of dust off the table and lowered myself onto a worn wooden stool. "Tarek's making a visit to the outskirts of Haren," I said, feigning nonchalance. "He's asked if I would like to go along."

"Oh, did he now?" Rhea saw right through my feigned indifference. Her eyebrows wiggled as a wicked grin rose on her freckle-splattered face. "And will there be any chaperones on this trip?"

"Don't give me that look, Rhea."

"Do there need to be any chaperones on this trip?"

"Rhea!"

She poked at my hip and cackled. "Ah, I see. You two looking for some time alone, then?"

A rosy blush spread along my cheekbones. "We'll see."

"Don't be coy with me. I've known you since you were a baby, tottering around this place in your underwear. You and that boy have been dancing around each other for nearly as long. Only an act of The Gods could keep you two from falling in love."

My throat turned dry. "Love is a big word. We're taking it slow for now."

"Tell that to the fool who hovers outside every afternoon staring at you like a lost puppy until your shift ends."

"Oh, that's not love, he's just imagining me tottering around in my underwear."

The smile lingered, but it faded as I noticed Rhea growing more thoughtful. She moved to the window, her silhouette framed by the harsh light filtering through the dust-caked glass. The quick wit and sparkle I was used to had softened, replaced by a pensive expression. Her gaze drifted towards the bustle of the street outside, where children darted between the legs of weary laborers.

"Tarek was telling me there's been more talk among the traders," I began, my voice hushed. "Rumors that if the drought doesn't break soon, the Council might—" I hesitated, the weight of what I was about to say making my throat tighten, "they might start rationing even more severely. Maybe even cut us off completely."

Rhea did not turn, but her posture stiffened. "Of course they will," she said, sharp and steady. "The Aquara will squeeze us until there's nothing left. It's always been the way with them, hasn't it? Like we're just numbers on a ledger."

I let out a slow breath, dizziness creeping back as I pressed my fingers to my temples. "It feels like a bad dream," I murmured. "We've lived through tough times before, but this... I can barely keep up at the center anymore. Every day more people come in and all I can do is offer them a bit of hope."

Rhea finally turned, her expression hardening into something unreadable. "They want us weak," she said, her voice low but fierce. "If we're too hungry, too thirsty, we can't fight back. We can't demand better when we're just trying to survive. We can't let them win, Solara. We have to show them we won't just roll over and accept this."

I looked up at Rhea. "What choice do we have? The Aquara control everything: the food, the water, the supplies. We can barely make it through the day as it is."

"There's always a choice," Rhea shot back, her eyes locking onto mine with an intensity that bordered on desperation. "We've been pushed to the edge, yes, but that's when people are most dangerous, when they have nothing left to lose. We need to start organizing, gathering those who are too angry to stay silent and too strong to just let this happen."

My gaze faltered. "And then what? Storm the Council? Demand they give us what little they have left? It sounds like a death sentence."

Rhea's jaw tightened, the words hanging in the air like a challenge. "Maybe it is, but living like this and just waiting for the end, that's no life at all. If we do nothing, they'll keep taking and taking until there's nothing left of us but bones and dust."

Neither of us spoke. Finally, I nodded, the gesture almost imperceptible. "You're right," I whispered. "It's not much of a choice, but it's the only one we've got."

Rhea's expression softened, a faint glimmer of that old twinkle returning. "We'll find a way," she said, not quite as confident as before. "We'll keep each other going. We've come this far, haven't we? Now, go on. Tarek's probably waiting with bated breath," she added with a mischievous smile.

I laughed, feeling the tension lift. "I'll try to keep him focused."

"You'll be fine getting home?" she asked.

"I'll be fine." I patted the twin daggers slung low on my hips. "Besides, I doubt many will risk the wrath of the mighty Arin Hawkthorne by getting handsy with his daughter." She smiled, warmth touching her face.

"He's a good man, your father. His retirement was a great loss to the Ignios Army."

"He tells me so every day," I said, winking.

She laughed and waved me off. "Take care, darling."

4

The Conversation

I returned Rhea's goodbye wave and spun on my boot heels towards the dodgier part of the city. Two hours remained on my shift and Paradise Row never made for a quiet afternoon as a healer. Without Rhea's presence distracting me, I was now acutely aware of how tense the city atmosphere had become. I clutched my cape tighter around my shoulders.

I hoped to get back to the safety of my family home. Aggressive boozehounds roaming the streets were nothing new, but today felt different. The Aquara wine that the Royal Guard had carted in for Solis Day was made to keep a drinker's spirits high for hours as they rode wave after wave of bliss. The effects lingered even a full day later.

Behind shuttered windows and drawn curtains, I caught nervous stares from women who had wisely decided to spend the day locked inside their houses, away from drunkards.

Some of these men would not be sobering up for days to come. There were so many of them that I had to weave through crowds, overhearing exchanges that ranged from sleazy to outright predatory. I ignored them, but rested my hands on the hilts of my blades, which occasionally glinted as they caught the sunlight. A warning.

"Well, aren't you a pretty thing," a voice leered from over my shoulder. Two men stumbled in my direction, close enough for me to catch the pungent reek of alcohol on their breath. Amber liquid sloshed in the tankards they carried. I swore under my breath. I had been too lost in my own thoughts to notice their approach.

My father would be disappointed. He had trained me better than to let my guard down.

It's never the enemy who attacks outright that will strike your killing blow, he had taught me. *It's the one who hides in the shadows and waits. The one who strikes when you've finally looked away. Those are the true predators to fear.*

I was fairly sure these sleazebags were more nuisance than predator, but I flexed my hands on my daggers nonetheless. If it came to it, I could vanish into the labyrinth of the city I knew so well, slipping through alleys and shadows. They would never be quick or clever enough to follow.

"I think we found a feisty one," the taller one said, jerking his chin toward my blades. "I do like it when they fight back," the shorter one taunted. He took a swig of wine and ran a tongue across his grimy teeth and I nearly lost my lunch.

The tall one pulled a fighting knife and twirled it in his palm. "Those are some heavy blades you've got there. Too heavy for a little lady like you to handle. I think you should hand those over to us."

"Along with any rations you've got on you," the shorter one added. He broke off from his friend to circle around my back. I sidestepped to cut off his path, though the movement put my back to a shadowed alley, which raised my hackles.

"Don't you boys have something better to do than harass women on their way home?"

"Harassing?" The shorter one clutched his chest with feigned hurt. "We're simply out celebrating this fine day after Solis."

I arched an eyebrow. "I doubt the Sun Gods would approve of this celebration."

His expression soured. "Then the Sun Gods can go freeze in the glaciers of hell."

The hair on the back of my neck rose. Blasphemy against the Sun Gods was punishable by death and the Aquara paid handsomely for citizens who were willing to turn on their own and report heretics. If this man would so brazenly insult the Sun Gods to my face, he had no intention of letting me walk away. I needed to get the hell out of here.

I took a few more steps back and dared a brief glance over my shoulder. I realized too late that the street I had backed myself into ended in a tall brick wall. My fingers twitched with the urge to pull my daggers. I could channel my father's training and use it to slice open their hands, cheeks or even their legs if they got too close. It would make for an easy escape without anyone ending up dead. Hopefully, it would not come to that, otherwise they would inevitably end up at the healers' center. *My healers' center.*

I had never taken a life before. My healer's vow was to help, not harm; my father's training was to survive at all costs. I did not want to be like the cruel Aquara, playing Gods by dealing out death like a hand of cards.

If my own life was on the line, *You must survive,* my father's words echoed in my ears. *At whatever cost, to whatever end. Survive first, mind the consequences later.*

It happened almost too quickly to see. The man lunged towards me, cool air skimmed my ribs as his dagger tip snagged my tunic and ripped a hole in it. My limbs flew in a choreographed war hymn my body could sing in its sleep.

It was all too easy to dodge their flailing, booze-affected swipes and land blow after blow of my own. A knee to the groin. The heel of a hand to the throat. A handful of dirt flung into their eyes. Each attack targeted to incapacitate them just enough.

The tall one screeched and buckled to his knees. Tears streamed down his cheeks as his eyes fought to clear the gritty debris. His friend lay on his back beside him, clutching his throat and gasping for air. "You're dead! Dead!"

"You said you wanted me to fight back." I stepped over their writhing bodies, swiping up their fallen knives and the broadswords at their hips. I did not have it in me to kill them, but I could at least make sure they thought twice before stealing from the next person they came across.

I kicked another cloud of dirt into their eyes, provoking a fresh round of howls. "Remember this the next time you think about randomly attacking a woman."

"Blessed Solis!" I said sweetly, as I dashed out of the alley and back onto the wider main road.

The commotion had begun to draw eyes in my direction. Heads craned to see who I was and what I had been doing. A gathering of four armed men started walking in my direction.

"You, woman!" one of them called out. "What's going on?"

Wonderful. If there was anything I needed less than two armed and angry men harassing me, it was six armed and angry men harassing me.

I spotted a nearby passage leading to a familiar set of alleyways. I crept toward it as I tugged my hood up over my head.

"You there!" the man called again. His steps quickened. "Stop where you are!"

"That bitch attacked me and stole my weapons!"

I winced. *Well, shit.*

The tall one staggered from the alley, finger extended my way. White-hot fury blazed in his eyes. "Stop her!"

I bolted for the alley as fiery adrenaline scorched through my veins.

I knew these paths well. This was not the poorest area of Sand City, but it was the seediest, the kind of place where you could chase any manner of sin. They called it Paradise Row, which was ironic or fitting, depending on what you sought.

As a healer, I had always been drawn to the most vulnerable of patients: an escort beaten bloody by her client, a desperate addict overdosing on drugs, a starving pickpocket who had lost a hand stealing from the wrong mark. My willingness as a healer to take on any call, no matter how dangerous or unsavory, made me a frequent visitor to Paradise Row.

The sound of distant shouting was gaining ground on me. I was too slow, weighed down by the stolen blades. I plunged down side paths at random—left, then right, then left again—and spotted a woman lounging against an open door, skirts hiked up and neckline plunged low.

"Free weapons," I said, panting as I rushed up to her. "Want them?"

Her eyes glazed over me with suspicion. "Nothing's free 'round here.'"

The crowd of voices grew louder.

"Fine." I jerked my chin over my shoulder. "Payment is keeping quiet about seeing me."

With a quick shrug, she scooped the blades from my arms and tossed them into a wooden chest inside her door.

"Don't show them the blades either," I warned. "Apparently drunk men don't like being disarmed by a woman."

She smirked knowingly, then nodded at an alley to the left. "Go that way."

I shot her a grateful smile and sprinted in the direction she had pointed. At my back, a woman's voice cried out, "That little brat took my knives, too! She went right! Catch her and bring her back here and I'll make it worth your while, boys."

Say what you want about the women of Paradise Row, but they certainly were loyal.

The darkness closed in around me as I raced deeper into the pathways. I could feel the weight of curious eyes peering out from shadowed doorways, watching me and assessing me. Some of the dilapidated buildings triggered memories of past visits, but I did not dare show a hint of recognition.

More voices drifted from down the path. I pressed my body against the wall to evade the few rays of speckled light. As a child, I had imagined that shadows were a tangible thing, a great blanket I could wrap around myself to hide from the world. I found myself doing the same now, silently begging my old friend, the darkness, to keep me veiled.

A flash of red caught my eye. A red I knew: bright, coppery and fluid, like poured silk. Tied as always into a knot at her nape.

I could have spotted my mother's distinctive hair in a crowd of thousands, but in this alley it was impossible to miss such a vibrant splash in a murky sea of browns and grays.

Her back was to me, her face hidden and her familiar cloak hung on her slender shoulders. Its rips and stains were the storybook of my childhood: tiny burns from our family hearth, a smear from young Kian's berry-stained hands and a mended tear from when a spooked horse had bucked her right into father's protective arms.

I froze in place, a surprised cry catching in my throat.

Seeing her here was not such a shock, as she also treated patients from Paradise Row. It was the man across from her who rendered me still.

He was everything she was not. Where my mother was petite, unassuming and draped in simple fabrics, this man was a demigod on proud display.

Even from a distance, it was obvious his clothes were of the finest materials. The black brocade of his floor-length overcoat, edged with intricate embroidery and gold-threaded roping, shimmered despite the murky light. Its sleek lines were perfectly tailored to fit every swell of his muscles. His boots were polished to a mirror shine, somehow immune to the Sand City grime that clung to everything I owned.

He towered above her by more than a foot, a feature he wielded over her like a weapon drawn and waiting to strike. He appeared a few years older than me and his face was angular and severe, emphasized by raven-black hair that was pulled back low and tightly and a scar that slashed across his olive skin. Its jagged lines splintered like lightning up from his collar, across his lips and over his narrowed eyes.

An Aquara.

Why was she here with him? She treated Aquara patients but never in Sand City and certainly not in Paradise Row. Other than the Royal Guard, their kind would not be caught dead in these parts, not unless they had come looking for trouble. Had he hunted her down? Had she seen something she should not have?

Was she in trouble?

My father's training kicked in once more. I scanned the man for potential threats. His features were tense and solemn, but not angry. Corded arms crossed over his impossibly broad chest. He had no guards or companions in sight. His only weapon was a sword strapped rather impractically to his back, its jewelled handle peeking out from above his shoulder. Only the Aquara would wear something so garishly better suited as jewelry than as a weapon fated to slice its way through muscle and bone.

The two of them were arguing. I could not make out the words, but I knew my mother's body language well enough. I had been on the wrong side of that pointed finger too many times. She and I shared something that the men of our family did not, a hot temper that could spontaneously ignite if provoked.

I flattened myself against the wall and tiptoed as close as I dared, then ducked behind a pile of empty wooden crates. As their argument intensified, their voices rose and carried across the alley.

"Out of the question," the man's voice rumbled.

"It was not a request," my mother answered.

"You don't give me orders, Liora."

"Need I remind you that one word from me and the entire realm will know that you—"

"No," he snapped. "I've already paid your extortion ten times over."

"And you'll keep paying it until lives are no longer in danger."

Extortion? What could my mother possibly have on an Aquara to make them bend to her will? She had been treating them for years, but the confidentiality between healer and patient was incredibly important. She was the model by which all healers in Haren were held. Surely she would never.

I leaned as far forward as I dared, squinting through the cracks in the crates.

The man uncrossed his arms and leaned his face down to hers. "Give me one good reason I should not kill you where you stand to be done with all of this."

My heart dropped to my stomach, but my mother was unbothered. She raised her chin in open defiance. "If I die, everyone will find out your secret. I've made sure of it."

The man's face remained a mask of composure, but his pale irises, slate blue with a touch of steel, glowed with icy fury. I shivered and gripped my dagger on reflex.

My mother spoke again in a gentler voice. "And because you know as well as I do that things are getting worse, and that helping me might be the only way to stop it."

They fell silent for a long moment. The scar-torn corner of his lip twitched into a frown. "If I do this, it must be tonight. There won't be another chance before…" He glanced around, then dropped his voice to a whisper.

I craned my neck, straining to pick up their hushed words. If only I could get a little closer.

"Eavesdropping will get you killed, child," a voice spoke from behind me.

I jolted at the unexpected sound and spun to find myself staring at the smirking face of an elderly woman. She leaned casually against the frame of a nearby doorway, her eyes so dark they seeemed black, her shoulders stooped with age.

"If you're going to listen in, at least make sure no one's watching your other side." Her voice rose and fell in a casual lilt with a smooth accent I could not place.

My mouth started moving before my mind could catch up. "I was not—I mean, I did not—"

"No use lying to me." The creases around her eyes bunched as she winked. "If your reasons for spying are worth knowing, then I know them already."

"I thought people in Paradise Row did not ask questions."

She shrugged. "Nothing wrong with being curious. It's what the answers will get you." Her dry, papery laughter ricocheted off the walls, filling every darkened corner.

I cringed, knowing the sound would carry to my mother and the mysterious stranger. A stolen glance confirmed that they had disappeared from sight.

"There go my answers," I muttered.

5

The Trio

SIX MONTHS LATER

"Solara."

It was less a name than a command, a hawkish summons that left room for nothing short of absolute obedience.

My shoulders pulled taut. This was not the voice of the loving father I knew, whose kind eyes and calloused hands would wrap me up in a chest-crushing embrace after a rough day. The man who, though we shared no blood, had been the best father I could have ever hoped for.

This was the voice of the man he had been before he became my father: the soldier who fought his way up the ranks of the Ignios Army, earning the highest rank ever given to a Haren citizen for bravery and leadership, both on and off the battlefield. The warrior whose name might have gone down in legend had he not walked away from it all for a quiet life with a penniless young mother and her two wild-spirited infants.

This was the voice of the Commander, which never meant anything good.

Kian lifted his head from the scrapyard junk he was working on and smirked in that infuriating, younger-sibling way. "Uh, oh, someone is in trouble…"

I rolled my eyes as I finished lacing my boots.

32

"And what have you done now?" His smile only widened, letting me have the last word. My brother was our father's most obedient soldier. If Kian ever found himself scolded by the Commander, it was only because he had taken the fall for me to spare me yet another lecture.

"So-la-ra," the voice boomed again, the three syllables stretching into a menacing dirge. "Get down here, now."

"Dead girl walking," Kian teased.

"Try to sound a little less thrilled about it, will you?" I tossed my waist-length waves into a sloppy braid and walked toward the main area, the weight of my weapons belt jangling with every step.

I bounded down the short hallway to the cool-aired chamber that served as the common room of our small home, sidestepping the teetering piles of books that seemed to fill every corner. My thoughts rummaged through the past few days, trying and failing to anticipate what had earned this particular reprimand.

Frankly, there were too many possibilities to count.

I skidded to a stop in front of my father and beamed my most believably innocent smile. My fist thumped to my chest in mock salute. "Present, Commander."

His eyes narrowed at my use of his former title. It was always a coin flip whether it would soothe or stoke his anger. Today, my odds were not looking good.

"Have you been taking your Emberberry?"

I fought the urge to cringe.

"Yes," I said, slowly and carefully.

"Every day?"

I shifted my weight. This was going to be ugly.

"I... may have missed a few days."

"How many days?"

"Things have been so busy. I've had a lot to do around here, the center is a mess and—"

"How many days, Solara." An order, not a question.

I sighed, then shrugged. "I'm not sure."

He crossed his arms with a deep-cut frown. Despite the wrinkles mapping their way across his features, he still looked every inch the fearsome warrior, with skin tanned and leathery from years under the Haren Sun and shoulders thick with muscle. "Well, I'm very sure. Do you know why I'm so sure?"

I swallowed a teasing response, managing instead to hold his gaze while shaking my head.

"Because I found this." He held up a crescent-shaped jar containing the small, purple berries. "It was inside my satchel. The satchel that hasn't been opened since I went to that meeting ten days ago."

For a brief moment, the argument played itself out in the theater of my head. I would complain that I was sick of taking the berries, that they made my brain fuzzy and my emotions dull. He would say those were necessary side effects, that the hallucinations which Emberberry prevented (symptoms of a disease I had inherited from my biological father) were far more severe than a clouded mind. I would let slip that I had actually stopped taking Emberberry weeks ago and still the visions had not returned yet. He would tell me that I was being reckless and immature and that my mother would be disappointed.

My mother.

That was a spiderweb I did not feel like getting snagged in.

Experience told me to cut my losses and give in. Even as I hung my head, working regret into my expression, a persistent voice cried out from deep inside of me. The call of my burning temper.

Fight.

"Thank you," I said with as apologetic a tone as I could muster. "I've been looking everywhere for that." I reached to pluck it from his grasp, but his other hand closed around my wrist.

"Solara, I need to be able to trust you."

Dueling waves of shame and irritation battled for release. I looked away, shoving them both down.

"I know things have been difficult since mother…" He trailed off, and I knew he was struggling to choose the right word. What could he say? "…Was taken? …Disappeared? …Left?"

We never had a funeral service for her. Never even admitted she might be dead.

Out of denial, naïveté, or just blind hope, we had convinced ourselves that she was simply away. She left on a trip that she had forgotten to mention. Visiting a distant patient who perhaps needed more help than she expected. Any day now, we would get a letter from her, apologizing profusely and explaining. Any day, she would walk back through the door.

For the first few weeks, I had almost believed it. Now, after so long, we did not talk about it. Swollen by months of silence, the truth had become too painful to touch.

"It's been hard for all of us, with her absent," he said.

Fight.

There it was again, the voice that plagued me. A harsh retort took form in my chest and I clenched my teeth to keep it in.

My father's expression softened. "You've done so much to help here at home and Naila told me how invaluable you've been at the center. I see the effort you're making and I appreciate it."

This was the Commander in action. The man who could see a soldier about to snap and reel them back in with kind words and an acknowledgement.

Normally, the ease with which he managed others' egos was inspiring. Now, watching him turn it on me so effortlessly only further rankled my nerves.

"I only worry for your health, sweetheart. If the illness comes back—"

"I'm fine," I cut in harshly. "I'm sorry. I'll take a dose today."

"Is there a reason you haven't been taking it?"

"I just... I've had a lot on my mind."

"How did that jar even get in my satchel?"

Because I can make my own decisions and I plan to shatter it in the pits of Ignios once I work up the nerve.

"I brought the box in last week. The jar must have fallen in then."
I marshaled a casual smile. "Father, I really need to get going or Kian and I will be late."

His drawn-out exhale made it clear he was unconvinced by my act, but he released my wrist.

I was almost to the door when his voice rang out again.

"Solara?"

I winced and glanced over my shoulder with eyebrows arched.

"I love you."

My temper dissolved at his gentle words. This generous man, who had given up everything all those years ago for my mother and us, was not the real reason for my anger. I tried desperately to remember that.

"Love you, too." I paused, then added with a wink, "Sir."

He gave a rumbling laugh and shooed me off. I grabbed my satchel and bounded out the front door before he could change his mind.

"So, he finally figured out you stopped taking the berries. What's it been, a month?"

I shushed my brother, nervously checking that Father was out of earshot. "I don't know what you're talking about."

Kian rolled his eyes and joined me as we walked the sandy streets.

I eyed him warily. "You knew?"

"Of course, I knew. You've been a different person since you stopped."

"I have?"

"Yes," he said, his tone suggesting the word was a gross understatement. "I'm surprised it took him this long to notice."

We walked in silence for a few minutes, listening to the crunch of gravel under our sandals, before I spoke again.

"Different how?"

"If I tell you, will you promise not to get mad at me for it?"

"No."

He snorted. "There's a perfect example."

I stopped and turned toward him with a glare. "Explain."

"You're angry. Moody. Stomping around, snapping at simple questions and treating everyone like an enemy."

He was not wrong. Lately, I had felt a growing outrage prodding me like a hot iron and the fuse of my temper trimmed alarmingly short. At first I had attributed it to my mother's absence, but she had been gone for months now.

It was in the weeks since swearing off Emberberry that things had really changed. With my mind now clear and my emotions no longer blunted to a dull edge, the injustices of the world grated on me in a way I found more and more impossible to ignore.

The snide comments from Kian's coworkers. The whispered gossip of the townsfolk. The violence and cold callousness of the Aquara guards.

My whole life, I had tried to convince myself I did not care what others thought or did. With the fog now lifting, I was beginning to realize that I very much did care and that I was sick of pretending otherwise.

I frowned as we fell back into step on the well-worn path. "Are you going to lecture me about it now, too? You want me to go back to being a quiet, obedient Solara?"

"You haven't been quiet or obedient for a day in your life." He nudged my side with his shoulder. "I trust your judgment. You're one of the best healers in the realm. Mother made sure of that. If you don't think you need Emberberry, then you know what you're doing."

I grumbled, though my chest warmed. "At least one member of my family trusts me."

"Father trusts you. He's just worried about you. We both are."

"I'm fine, I swear. If the symptoms come back, I'll start taking it again." I sighed and hooked an arm through his, tugging him close. "And you're right. I have been angrier lately. Though I'm not sure if it's the Emberberry or..." I waved a hand vaguely around me, motioning to the world beyond. "Everything."

"I know." His voice grew quiet. "Do you think we'll ever see her again?"

I wanted to say yes. I wanted to assure him that all would be well, and that this was only a brief hiccup in our otherwise ordinary lives. More than that, I wanted to believe it myself. Kian had always been the one person I could never lie to, even when the truth was too painful to bear.

"I don't know," I said, honestly. "I thought I would feel it somehow, deep down, if she were really gone. Father seems convinced she's still out there, but she vanished without even saying goodbye or sending a letter. " I squeezed my eyes shut to fight off the dread seeping into my thoughts. "She's always had her secrets, but this is unusual, even for her."

"And your investigation turned up nothing?"

I stiffened. "It's not *nothing*. I found out she'd been going to the Palace more frequently the week before she disappeared. A Royal Aquara was unwell, and they had called on her almost every day. Naila's been going in her place since then, but she swears she hasn't seen or heard anything unusual."

"What about that Aquara man you saw her talking to?"

A memory flashed through my mind. Dark features cut with a scar and piercing eyes. I saw his face every time I closed my eyes and heard his low voice whispering in my ears when my mind wandered. In the months since seeing him I had searched for some sign of him, hoping he might know something–anything, that could help me find her.

I had made the mistake of asking a few of the townsfolk, but I saw the scorn in their eyes when I described my mother following a wealthy Aquara man into Paradise Row. Rumors that she had fallen pregnant out of wedlock and fled in shame spread like wildfire soon after.

The reminder of it brought my anger roaring back to the surface. That would never be my mother, not for a thousand reasons. My mother was a woman of honor, strength and humility. She had earned her place among the Aquara healers, rising through the ranks to become one of Haren's most respected and capable practitioners. We learned early on how to make do with whatever we had. She taught me how to fashion bandages from palm leaves and grind the shells of the tough exoskeletons of Silkwing Beetles to extract a balm that soothed wounds like nothing else. We never relied on anyone. I knew she would never let herself be vulnerable, not even to the man who could have swept her off her feet if she had let him.

"I'm still looking for him," I responded tightly. "But I'm not giving up. I'll find her, Kian."

"I believe you. If anyone can, it's you."

We walked in silence again, the crushing weight of her absence making the air around us heavy and hard to breathe.

"You don't have to walk me to work, you know." Sharpness edged into Kian's normally mild voice and I wondered if my newfound irritability had been rubbing off on him.

"What kind of sister would I—"

"—Yeah, but I'm eighteen now. I can handle myself."

"But you're still my little brother."

"Solara, listen—"

A lighthearted voice interrupted our spat. "Haven't you learned by now, there's no winning an argument against the great Solara Hawkthorne?"

I smirked. Kian groaned.

"Thank you, Tarek, I've been telling him that for years," I said to the shaggy-haired man swaggering toward us.

Tarek flung an arm around my shoulders and grinned down at Kian. "Whatever it is, take my advice and accept defeat. She's especially relentless when it comes to you, kid."

Kian bristled. "I'm not a kid. And this is none of your concern."

I snaked my arm around Tarek's waist and squeezed his side in a silent plea to back off.

Kian was straddling the cusp of boyhood and manhood, which had become a growing sore spot. Young kids in Sand City finished school at fourteen and carved out paths for themselves shortly after. I had done the same, beginning my healer work with Mother five years ago.

Tarek's constant teasing did not help. With no siblings of his own, Tarek fancied himself an adoptive big brother, an role Kian had never quite warmed to.

Tarek held his free hand up in mock surrender. "Sorry. Family business. I'll keep my mouth shut."

"Unlikely," I joked, though I shot him an appreciative look as we turned onto the main road leading to Sand City.

"How's work?" he asked Kian. "Are the factory managers treating you with kindness and respect?"

Kian wrinkled his nose at Tarek's dripping sarcasm. "All they talk about is who will take over once the King of Aquara dies. They're even taking bets on it. The man's on his deathbed, and they're circling like vultures."

"Deathbed?" I frowned. "The King is dying?"

"You haven't heard?" Kian's lips parted in an incredulous stare. "Solara, he's been sick for months. They say he's nearly gone now. He lies in bed and stares at the ceiling, just waiting for the end."

"How sad," I murmured as I thought of the many patients I had treated in similar states. Kian was still staring at me with a strange look and I arched an eyebrow. "What?"

"You really did not know?"

"How would I have known?"

"Because Mother was treating him."

"Our mother?" I blinked. "She was treating King Thalor?"

Tarek matched my brother's odd expression. "What did you think she was doing up at the Palace every day?"

I shook my head. "This doesn't make sense. If his condition was that serious, why not call in a healer from the Godsdamned healing realm itself?! With their healing technology…"

Tarek shrugged. "Maybe it's not something an Aquara healer can fix. I once read in a manuscript from the Relic District that sometimes the Sun Gods themselves will decide it's time for the Crown to change hands, even if they're young and healthy."

"If that's the case, why not simply strike him dead?" I asked. "Letting the man waste away slowly for months seems needlessly cruel."

"Maybe people's fates are as corrupt and soulless as those who wield power," Tarek muttered. I shivered at the coldness in his voice. He pulled me in tighter, giving my shoulder a squeeze.

Tarek did not just dislike the Aquara, he despised them. Some nights we would lay out by the water to stare at the stars and he would tell me of his dream that one day Haren would be free of Aquara rule, united into a single nation as it had been so long ago. I had always dismissed it as a fantasy, but lately there had been a spark in his eyes when he spoke of it, a sense of certainty that this day was coming and that we would be alive to see it.

"Do the Aquara really have no idea who the next Crown will be?" I asked.

"None," Kian answered. "In theory, the Sun Gods will choose the most powerful Aquara, but measuring their power is more art than science."

"Who's the betting pool favorite?"

"Prince Darian, the King's nephew. He's incredibly powerful, no matter how you measure it."

I felt Kian tense beside me, and his gait faltered, though he said nothing. I shot him a questioning look. "Have you met him?"

His lips formed a tight line. "No, but his sister Vira—Princess Viriana, I mean—came to the factories one day to discuss some trade agreements. She seemed... really nice." If his splotchy, blushing cheeks had not betrayed him, his casual use of her nickname would have.

"Really nice, huh?" I teased. "Is Viriana also really... pretty?" A mischievous smile lit up my face.

He tried not to react. "She's Aquara. They're all really pretty."

"Let me rephrase. Do I need to hunt Viriana down and threaten to slip Rosebane into her morning tea if she breaks my little brother's heart?"

"By the Sun Gods," Kian hissed, his head whipping around to look for eavesdroppers. "Do you have a death wish? You can't walk around threatening to murder members of the Royal Family."

"I did not say I would kill her." I shrugged. "In the right dose, Rosebane just makes you a very teeny tiny bit, temporarily insane."

"That's not any better, Solara!"

"What? They used to call it Gods' Horn because those who survived it claimed they could talk directly to the Gods." I could not help my smile at my brother's exasperated groan. "Just imagine, pretty Viriana could have a nice chat with the Sun Goddess herself."

"I need to leave before you two get me executed." Kian broke off and headed back toward the house. "Try not to plot any more royal assassinations in public, please."

"We'll take it under consideration," I said cheerfully, waving goodbye.

Tarek grinned. "No promises."

6

The Visit

I was at the healers' center finishing up my duties for the day when a petite blonde woman burst through the door. She wore a deep blue velvet dress embroidered with delicate silver swirls and jeweled rings that glittered along her pale fingers. Her features were strained as she scanned the room with fear-stricken eyes.

An Aquara.

"Liora! I'm looking for Liora Hawkthorne!" she wheezed, her chest heaving for breath. "Where is she?"

The sound of my mother's name sent a sharp swell of grief surging through me. "She's... unavailable."

"I was told to get Liora Hawkthorne. It's urgent! You have to hurry!" Her hands trembled.

"She isn't here, but I'm sure we can help. Can you tell me what's happened?"

"The water... The Princess went limp... she's sick. Badly. Please! Please come with me."

A professional calmness settled over me as my training instincts kicked in. I did what a composed Naila or my mother would do. "How did she get sick?" I asked in a confident and reassuring voice. "Is she breathing? Is she conscious? Responsive?"

"She... she drank the water. Her face went blue... She could not breathe, I think. Please, hurry!"

Without a word, my gaze met Naila's. An unspoken understanding passed between us. We nodded in unison, reaching for our satchels. I stuffed mine with gauze, splints and jars of various remedies, grabbing anything that might be useful. Better to be overprepared than to risk missing something important.

"You stay," I said. "I'll handle this."

"I'm coming with you," she cut in. "You can't deal with this on your own."

"Naila, please," I paused. "I've got this."

She hesitated, eyeing me nervously. "But your mother..."

"Isn't here." The words came out more bitterly than I had intended. "You can take it up with her when she comes back."

Naila pursed her lips but said nothing more.

"What's your name?" I asked, turning back to the Aquara girl, who looked as though she would spill the contents of her stomach any second.

"El..Eloisa"

"Eloisa, I'm Solara." I paused, laying a hand on her velvet-covered shoulder. "Everything is going to be fine."

I suddenly realized that this was the first time I had ever touched an Aquara and certainly the longest I had sustained a conversation with one. To feel the soft fabrics of her dress… the intricate silver embroidery must have cost more than I would earn in a month.

All my life I had been sheltered from Aquara, raised on a steady diet of myth and fear. I had learned to imagine them to be something monstrous. Cold-blooded, ruthless and incapable of empathy or any human decency.

Yet this pale girl shaking with fear seemed so utterly *normal*. So normal, I even questioned whether I might enjoy her company. If not for her appearance, she could easily have passed for a healer from the center or a Relic from Haren's Knowledge District.

"Thank you," she breathed, some tension in her features easing at my words.

I finished gathering the medical supplies and we hurried out onto the dirt path that wound away from the healers' center. There, several Aquara guards stood in front of a vehicle that looked like it was forged from brass and steel. The guards' armor glistened with interlocking plates that provided both mobility and protection. Each piece was adorned with symbols of their order, etched in silver and highlighted with deep blue accents that caught the light with every movement.

The vehicle itself was a marvel of craftsmanship. It hovered silently, its sandy hue blending seamlessly with the landscape. Its surface was as smooth as polished stone, made from a lightweight alloy that seemed to absorb and reflect sunlight. The edges were tapered to sharp points, giving it a predatory look. Below, the thrusters emitted a faint, bluish glow that cast an eerie light on the sands as it hovered effortlessly a few feet above the ground. It was like nothing I had ever seen. A Sand Skimmer.

The sound of whispers roared around us as people curiously approached to take a better look at the vehicle. This was the kind of technology a Haren could only dream of seeing—the final product of their hours of backbreaking labor in the Technology District to create machine parts that would only be assembled in Aquara. The steering wheel was made of steel mined from the Tarnak Caves in Haren. The plush seats were upholstered with hand-woven fabric originating from the skilled artisans of Haren, who toiled for weeks perfecting the exquisite silk material.

We both rushed toward the vehicle, its entrance flanked by two guards. As I stepped inside, it took all of my self-control to hold back my astonishment. The interior was stunning. The cockpit had a holographic display flickering softly, showing detailed readouts of terrain, weather conditions and what I assumed were navigational routes. The control panel was an array of touch-sensitive buttons, centered around a joystick of limitless maneuverability.

Eloisa's voice snapped me out of my thoughts.

"It was my fault," she said in a shaky whisper so low only I could hear. "I was the one who poured her that glass of water." Her voice broke.

I grabbed her hand, gave it a light squeeze, and said, "Accidents happen, Eloisa."

"When my brother and I were little," I began, "I stuck some Scarwort in his bag. I only meant to tease him with the smell, but on our way to school, a wild snake caught the smell and attacked him. It sank a fang right through his calf. We were all alone and I thought he was going to die right in front of me... all for a foolish joke." My stomach clenched at the memory of holding my brother's bleeding body in my arms while screaming for help. "Then I was scared that, even if he did survive, he would hate me forever. I was also convinced my parents would never forgive me."

Eloisa's panic faded at the momentary distraction. "Did he survive?"

"He did."

"Did he forgive you?"

"He got to stay home from school for weeks and eat all the sweets he wanted. It was the greatest time of his life. He *thanked* me."

A faint smile reached her lips. "And your parents?"

"They weren't happy, but they knew my heart. They knew I would never hurt him on purpose." I squeezed her hand. "That's what family's all about. Knowing you are loved even when you make stupid mistakes."

She said nothing as I watched a flurry of mixed emotions cross her face. A glimmer of hope was beginning to replace the heavy cloud of guilt she had been carrying.

When the Sand Skimmer finally stopped, I was at last able to take note of my surroundings. I could see the Royal Palace through an open set of towering metal gates.

"Solara," Eloisa's voice sliced through my thoughts, grounding me in the present. I looked up to find her standing ahead, flanked by two guards. They exchanged a brief glance before stepping aside to let us pass. Without wasting a second, we moved toward the gates.

Eloisa exhaled sharply, her voice low and urgent. "I know a shortcut that'll get us there faster, but you can't tell anyone about this. Ever."

"Okay, I promise."

The moment the words left my mouth, she veered off the path, darting into the dense forest that surrounded the Palace. After a few minutes of clambering over tangled roots and ducking beneath low branches, an enormous wall smothered in leafy vines emerged from the forest. It blended so perfectly into the vegetation that, in the dark, I might have slammed straight into it.

Eloisa felt around the wall, mumbling quietly to herself as she searched. "Here! Follow me. Quickly!"

She pulled back the foliage to reveal a hole barely large enough for an able body to pass through. She peered through the opening and glanced around before motioning for me to go on.

A secret entrance.

One by one we crawled through, our satchels clinking as they dragged along the ground. As I breathed in the sweet fragrance of florals and fresh herbs, I realized we had entered a large garden. A rustling sound caught my attention as Eloisa drew the curtain of rope-like vines, slipping it back into place.

Turning around to face the Palace, I nearly choked. From Sand City, I had only ever seen faint glimpses of the Royal Palace, a crown of spires peeking over the city to keep watch on us from afar. I had always imagined it to be some imposing stone fortress, a building as fearsome and impenetrable as the Aquara themselves.

What stood before me was something else entirely.

It seemed to be made not of stone or metal, but of light itself. Its structure rose and fell in sharp waves, the walls radiating an ethereal shimmer, like starlight given physical form. A mass of towering steeples disappeared into the sky, visible only by the faint sheen of reflected blue.

A thin layer of water streamed down the entrance walls, creating a shimmering curtain that caught the light in a dazzling display of colors. A fountain in front sprouted constantly, its crystalline jets gleaming in the sunlight, creating rainbows in the mist that floated around it. It was a powerful reminder of what this realm owned. Far from frightening or imposing, it was the most beautiful thing I had ever seen.

Just as my jaw fell slack, Eloisa gave me a gentle nudge and ushered me toward the grand entrance of the Palace.

Before I knew it, we were already climbing the marble steps to a set of giant arched doors. I took a mental picture of my surroundings, knowing that this was probably the first and last time I would be here.

While I had told Naila with rather unshakable confidence that I could handle this situation, the grandeur of the Palace and the seriousness of the situation suddenly made me question whether I was capable at all. I had packed every antiseptic herb I could think of, but Eloisa's description of the girl's face turning blue suggested something far more serious than a routine cut or burn I was used to treating during my healer shifts. A knot of fear tightened in my stomach.

As I entered the Palace, a large gold crest at the top of the archway caught my attention. It was an enormous design in the shape of a shield, gleaming blindingly in the sunlight. The crest depicted the face of a muscular creature with powerful and commanding features. Its face was framed by a thick mane that made it look both regal and fearsome. The detailed features made the creature's eyes appear almost lifelike, its gaze penetrating and wise, as if silently judging my worthiness to step further into the Palace.

The splendor did not end when I stepped past the door.

If Sand City was a gloomy array of stone and dirt, this place was an artist's palette. Buttery yellows, flaming reds and oranges, watery blues and mossy greens painted the interior, woven into tassel-edged rugs and towering tapestries that stretched taller than my house. Lifelike paintings in gilded frames adorned the walls, each one lit by a hovering orb of warm golden light. Several long tables overflowed with fruits, pastries and steaming dishes whose aromas wafted through the chamber. There were real fruits that were hydrated, plump and luscious, not the slabs of pulp we ate daily in Sand City.

Just as my mouth started to salivate, the moans of a pained young Aquara echoed through the corridors. As we ascended a flight of stairs and stopped at a door, the source of the sound became clear. A young girl lay limp in her bed, her frail form cradled by an Aquara man.

"I brought a healer," Eloisa said, pushing her way through the throng. "Move! Move!"

The women parted, forming a pathway leading to the girl. Her skin was pale and clammy, her breath shallow and labored. Dark circles shadowed her eyes and her face was contorted in pain.

She was held closely in the arms of a man who was gently murmuring to her in a hushed and soothing tone. His ebony hair had fallen free from its binding and obscured his features. The girl stared up at him, her face an unnatural shade of blue. A constellation of red, swollen blotches had blossomed across her chest, snaking up her neck like a creeping vine. A thin trickle of blood ran from her nose, stark against her discolored skin.

Blotchbane.

My knowledge of poisons quickly identified her symptoms as those of Blotchbane, the rare and lethal toxin derived from a plant native to the arid regions of Haren. As children, we were always warned to steer clear of the plant. The question was how this Aquara girl had come into contact with such a deadly substance.

I knelt at her side and gently reached for her arm. She flinched, and the man beside her gave me a scorching glare.

"Hello," I said to her softly, conjuring up my well-practiced calm. "I'm a healer, and I'm here to help you. Can you tell me what hurts?"

"Isn't it obvious?" the man interrupted. I ignored him, my gaze locked onto my patient.

"My throat, my whole body," she answered. Her voice was quiet but raspy, her eyes bright and her breathing steady. All good signs.

"Can you try moving your arm?" I asked.

"No," the man shot back on her behalf. "She's clearly paralyzed."

His presence was demanding, but I refused to let my focus waver. I had enough experience working around patients' overbearing family members. Just because this one was an entitled, rich and powerful Aquara would not keep me from doing my job.

"Can you speak?" I repeated to her.

The girl shook her head weakly, wincing with the effort. This was exactly the sort of thing my mother had not taught me yet.

I dug into my satchel and retrieved a large stoppered flask. "I'm going to give you something to help with the pain. Can you tell me your name?"

"I—I'm Vira," she stammered.

"You may call her Princess Viriana," the man corrected, ratcheting up the intensity of his stare.

My stomach sank as the name rolled off her tongue. Princess Vira—Viriana. The very same Aquara Princess my brother had blushed at the mere mention of.

My head tilted as I assessed her through a completely new lens.

"Nice to meet you, Princess Viriana," I said politely. I could tell the man's unease with my casual tone. "My name is Solara. Can you take a big drink of this for me?"

The Princess's brow furrowed as she focused on the vessel. "What is it?"

Questioning mystery liquids from strangers—smart girl. No wonder Kian liked her.

"Silverworm. It's made from a lovely white flower that grows near the shore." I brought my face close to hers and winked. "Don't worry, there's no real worms in it."

She gave the faintest of smiles and the man's tightly coiled posture finally eased. As I tilted the flask to her lips, I scanned her for wounds and spotted red blotches all over her petite body.

I tucked away a stray lock of hair that had fallen over her face. "Soon you're going to feel much better, Princess Viriana. The Silverworm needs a few minutes to take effect, but I'll wait here with you until then. Would that be alright?"

She nodded again. A tear escaped from her midnight blue eyes, leaving a wet track along her cheek. Her lower lip began to quiver. She turned her face to the man whose arms still held her close. "I'm s-sorry. I should not have drunk the water."

He cupped her face in his hand, brushing away her tears with his thumb. "You did not know. Don't ever apologize for that."

The man's gentle voice was a stark contrast to the harsh tone he had used with me. I finally dared to bring my eyes up to study his face.

Instantly, every thought flushed from my head.

Olive skin. Grey eyes. A long, uneven scar. Raven-black hair.

Him.

It was *him.*

I had scoured Sand City for months for clues that might lead me to the Aquara man I had seen arguing with my mother the day she disappeared. Now here he was, inches away from me, the one person with the answers I sought. The man whose secrets my mother had used against him.

The man who might have killed her to keep them quiet.

My eyes darted to the jeweled hilt rising over his shoulder, the very same he had worn that day in the alley. I blinked a few times and shook my head, as if the movement might reveal it was all an illusion.

He was now so close in front of me.

He must have noticed me staring because his attention flicked up.

Perhaps for only a millisecond, a fleeting glimmer of recognition seemed to connect us.

It was gone in a second, locked behind two masks.

I immediately looked away and busied my hands with my bag.

"Have we met?" he asked, his tone curious.

"No," I said too quickly.

The man went still and I felt the weight of his stare again. This time it took all my effort not to meet it with my own.

He knew.

Somehow, I felt certain he knew what happened to my mother.

The thought made my chest tense up again. As anger and fear swelled up in me, I could feel a slight tremor take a hold of my hands.

Right then and there, I could have lunged at him and demanded answers.

Fight.

The voice. The same one that had hounded me this morning in the kitchen with my father, charged through my head like a raging bull.

My fingers tightened around the flask, overcoming the tremor. "How does your chest feel?" I asked through gritted teeth.

"I can't feel anything. Does that mean it's working?"

I applied pressure to her arm, gradually moving closer to where her flesh had begun to redden and swell. She gave no reaction. "Good. Now I'm going to add a salve. It will probably burn, so you'll have to take some deep breaths for me."

I rolled my shoulders back and tried to steady myself with a few shaky breaths.

Fight.

I clenched my jaw and channeled the energy coursing through my blood into my hands as I gripped her delicate shoulder. Just as I was about to lather a swab of the white paste, the man spoke.

"Wait," he interrupted. "Shouldn't I do this?"

"Are *you* the healer?" I shot back. I refused to look at him for fear that his condescending expression might make me lose control. How dare he suggest I need his help to do my job?

"Princess Viriana, close your eyes, take a deep breath."

Princess Viriana eyed my hands nervously for a moment, then her eyelids fluttered closed. Her chest rose once, then fell.

The man held up a hand. "Are you sure I should not—" This time, I ignored him.

As soon as I lathered her skin, she howled in pain. Once it was all done, Princess Viriana gasped and recoiled away from me. The man tucked her snugly against his chest. "You're safe," he assured her, his tone gentle once again.

"You did perfectly, Princess," I said. "That was the only scary part. The rest will be easy." I coaxed her out of his arms and began treating her, wrapping her blotches in bandages.

Once finished, I gestured for Princess Viriana to stand. I realized with frustration that, having never seen these kinds of blotches before, I had no idea how long her arm would take to heal or if it would even heal at all. Mother would have known, but I was out of my depth. Still, my pride kept me silent and composed. I was not going to show any self-doubt before this man, not after he had questioned my skills.

I started to excuse myself and pack my things when I noticed the Princess swaying on her feet. Her face was drained of color, her eyes now cloudy and glazed.

"Princess?" I asked slowly. "Are you okay?"

Her eyes rolled back into her head. With a short, rattling breath, she collapsed into the man's arms, and her body went still.

7

The Light

"Vira!" the man shouted. His sharp panic cut through me like a scalpel. He gripped the back of her head as her body slumped to the ground. "Something's wrong. Help her!"

I had missed something crucial.

In my mind, the world turned into an empty stillness. A numbness overwhelmed me. Sounds were silenced. Lights dimmed and the room faded to black. The girl lay before me, unconscious.

I dropped to my knees, my hands moving as if by their own free will. I shoved the man away, ripped off his protective hold and checked her pulse, her eyes, her breath. My palms roamed her clothes in search of signs of injury.

The shade of her face deepened to an unnatural blue as her body convulsed violently. Her limbs jerked uncontrollably and her torso arched with each spasm, as if seized by invisible forces. Blood seeped steadily from her nose, mingling with the swelling blotches on her skin.

I pulled a jar from my bag and forced a scoop of the mixture under Princess Viriana's tongue, offering silent prayer to whichever Sun Gods were listening. There were no external injuries. It was something internal attacking her system.

I shifted her body to look at her face. Her skin had turned ashen and clammy.

"Come on, Princess," I growled beneath my breath.

I should have seen this. I had missed the signs, too distracted by the man, while a girl had been slipping away right in front of me.

I thought of Kian and the way his eyes lit up when he talked about her. "She's really nice," he had said. So few in this miserable world had ever been nice to him. If she died at my hands, I would not be able to live with it on my conscience."

"Fight," I demanded, willing every shred of conviction I could muster. "I need you to fight, Princess."

Fight, the voice inside me echoed.

A strange feeling stirred in my chest. My hands tingled with a sensation that was at once freezing cold and scorching hot. It was almost painful, but I did not dare pull away.

My palms, covering the blood-soaked gauze on her chest, suddenly began to emit a soft glow. It was powerful and beyond anything explainable. I would need time to process it later. All I could do was hunch my body over hers to hide it.

"Yes," I whispered. "Fight, Princess Viriana. Fight."

The light beneath my hand grew stronger. It now blazed with a radiant, silver and moonlight-like glow.

The Princess's eyes flew open.

Her chest swelled with a gasp as she jolted upright. Her lips were bright pink, and her sapphire eyes sparkled.

Motionless and silent, we stared at each other.

My awareness of the world around me gradually began to return. I became acutely aware that all the eyes in the room were turned on us. I looked down at the injury and carefully peeled back the gauze.

My eyes could not believe what they were seeing.

The blotches and the blood were gone. Not faded or healed, but gone. As if it had never happened.

I removed the dressings completely, but there was still nothing visible, not even a scratch.

Without fully knowing why, I clamped the gauze back down to hide the pristine skin.

"H-how do you feel?" I stammered.

Princess Viriana's dumbstruck expression mirrored my own. "Good, I think. What... what happened?"

I shook my head, struggling to form words. "You were... bleeding and shaking. But you—you're alright. It's alright now."

A small group of Aquara women congregated around us. Their hands scrambled for the Princess, stroking her hair, her arms, cooing words of reassurance and murmuring among themselves in disbelief. I retreated from the crowd, confused and feeling lightheaded.

I looked at my scarlet-drenched hands. The wound had been real. There had been blood. I had seen it and felt its warmth on my hands. In the depths of my soul, I knew that something extraordinary had happened. Something beyond any healer's comprehension of the world.

As I continued to retreat from the crowd, I bumped into a small body. It was Eloisa. Our eyes locked.

"That was incredible," she gushed. She looked at me in awe, as if she had been the one I had saved. "Did you—"

"Is there somewhere I can wash up?" I interrupted. My lungs struggled to draw every breath. My body was drained. I felt weightless.

Eloisa recoiled at the sight of my bloody, shaking hands. "Um... yes, of course." She led me to the hallway and pointed. "Last door on the right."

I nodded in thanks and staggered forward as the Palace spun wildly around me. Halfway down the corridor, my knees wobbled, threatening to give way. I leaned against a nearby wall and closed my eyes.

The silvery glow of my palms had faded, but I could still sense the phantom tingling in my palms.

After a few torturous minutes, I was able to settle my weight back onto my feet. My breathing steadied, my pulse eased from a thunderous gallop.

I pushed off the wall with my regained strength. As I turned towards the washroom, I felt an energy holding me back. A firm hand clasped around my elbow and turned me around, bringing me face-to-face with the man who'd been at Princess Viriana's side.

"Where are you going?" he demanded.

I was in no mood for it. "If you value that hand, you'd best remove it from my arm,"

His gaze scanned me from head to toe. I could almost hear his assessment of my height, build, and daggers, dismissing that I posed a threat. The arrogance of it almost made me smile. Proud men had underestimated me before, always to their detriment.

"Hand. Off." I snapped. I angled my body to conceal my palm as it inched toward my blade hilt.

He held my stare for a few tense seconds before finally letting me go. It was his way of reminding me that he was the one in control, not me.

"How did you do that for the Princess?" he asked, his tone deceptively soft.

"I'm a healer. It's my job."

"The light you made back there..."

"That was Princess Viriana. I did nothing."

He looked unconvinced, scanning my face in search of an answer I could not provide.

Here he was, finally standing before me, the man I had been searching for months to find. My lips parted with the urge to ask him about my mother, but a gut instinct held my tongue.

I could not shake the feeling that asking him those questions would open a door I could never again close. Judging from the knife-edge sharpness of his voice and the suffocating intensity of his presence, this was not someone I wanted involved in my life. If he had been willing to kill my mother to keep her silent, what might he do to me if he believed I knew his secrets too?

He glanced over his shoulder at the empty corridor, then dropped his voice to a whisper. "Where are your parents from? Your father. Is he from Ignios?"

My thoughts crashed in a jumbled frenzy. How could he have known? Did he mean the Commander, or did he mean my birth father? Was it possible he knew me?

My expression seemed enough of an answer for him. He lifted his eyes to the ceiling. "Wonderful," he mumbled.

"What? How did you—?"

"You should not be here." He jerked his chin toward my daggers. "Non-Aquara visitors aren't permitted to carry weapons in the Royal Palace." He emphasized the word "Royal," letting it hang in the air like a sharp jab. It was as if he were reminding me of my place in their hierarchy—below them.

My temper flared anew. The Aquara can kill us at the flick of a finger, and he was implying Harens are the threat?

"What's the problem?" I bit back. "Scared of a Haren woman?"

"Hardly." His tone was emotionless and matter-of-fact. "Haren or not, you'd be dead before that dagger left its sheath."

For a foolish second, I considered putting his claim to the test.

"Why do my daggers concern you, then? I thought flimsy Haren weapons could not pierce Aquara skin."

"They can't—except our children's." Immediately, his features tightened, as if chastising himself for revealing a weakness.

"You think I would hurt a *child?*" I hissed.

He opened his mouth to respond but fell silent as I stormed forward. I poked my blood-coated finger into the solid wall of his chest, getting a small thrill of satisfaction as his eyes widened in surprise.

"If I wanted to hurt those children, I would have let your Princess bleed to death. I could have stayed home and let her meet her end. Instead, I saved her and this is how you thank me?"

A muscle twitched in his jaw. For a moment, I thought he was going to say something.

My lips curled. "If you'll please excuse me, I need to wash up. It seems I made a mess while saving *your* people." I spun on my heel and marched away.

It was not until I was in the washroom and heard the soft click of the lock sliding into place that I slumped to the ground and burst into tears. It felt good to finally let go. At one point, I choked with laughter at the miserable picture of myself, covered in blood and weeping on the floor of the most extravagant room I had ever set foot in.

The washroom was half the size of my family's home, its domed ceiling hand-painted with the image of a swirling evening sky. Light twinkled through the stars dotting the expanse of sapphire and obsidian whorls.

In an alcove, a circle of solid, gold-plated washbasins surrounded a fountain of the Sun Goddess emerging from a bubbling pond. Rows of cut-crystal jars containing soaps and perfumes lined shelves along the wall. There was even a hearth, still aglow with the embers of a dying fire, warming a pyramid of soft, fluffy towels.

My eyes dropped to the dark marble floor, its white and gold veins swirling around a trail of bloody smears that led directly to me. "Great," I muttered to myself. "Just perfect."

I wiped away a tear with the back of my hand. I was not even sure why I was crying. Maybe it was the way that insufferable Aquara man had looked at me, like I was a mere bug he could crush at his own leisure. Or maybe I was just a daughter who missed her mother.

Seeing him dragged me back to moments in time: the image of the crinkle of her eyes on the cursed afternoon when I last saw her with him in the street. Or a more pleasant, distant memory of her sweet laughter while we walked into town together, arms linked.

Until now, I had not allowed myself to accept that she might truly be gone. For my family's sake, I had always played along with the fantasy that she might still be alive somewhere and would eventually come home.

Sitting in the fancy Palace surrounded by Aquara, the very situation my mother had spent a lifetime trying to keep me away from, felt like some kind of closure. A goodbye of sorts.

Life after Liora Hawkthorne.

"Five minutes," I told myself. "You get five minutes to feel sorry for yourself. Then you get up, and you get back to work."

I tilted my head back against the cold stone wall and closed my eyes. It was time to turn the page and move on.

8

The Prince

The rest of my afternoon duties took me on a tour of Sand City, making house calls to a number of poor families. By the time I returned to the healers' center, day had melted into evening, and the trainees had departed for the night, leaving Naila and me alone in the empty quiet. Naila scribbled the day's notes into our records while I finished bottling a new batch of Willowmoss salve.

"Was everything alright this morning with the Aquara girl?" Naila called out.

"Yes, just a poisoning," I replied, capping the last bottle.

"Oh."

A moment of silence stretched between us. "The Aquara weren't what I expected," I said.

Naila glanced up. "What do you mean?"

I paused my work. "They seemed almost... *normal*."

"Well, they may be genetically stronger and taller, but the same blood runs in our veins after all. What did you expect them to be like?"

I shrugged. "Cruel. Soulless."

"They can be, sometimes. I suppose concern for a loved one is universal. Even the wildest beasts can be gentle when their young are in danger."

The panicked voice of the mysterious man calling for help as Princess Viriana collapsed in his arms replayed in my ears. I could still vividly picture the gentle caress with which he wiped away her tears and the kindness he showed her.

Until today, I would never have imagined them capable of any kind of love, kindness or empathy.

"That reminds me," Naila interrupted my thoughts. "The King's nephew came by this afternoon while you were out. He asked me to give you his thanks."

I frowned. "You mean Eloisa?"

"No, not Eloisa. Prince Darian."

I froze.

"Was Prince Darian at the Royal Palace this morning?"

"You really don't know the Royals at all, do you?" Naila grinned. "Solara! You were sitting right beside him, apparently. He is the patient's brother. They're the King's niece and nephew."

Oh, Gods. *Oh, Gods.*

The man I had been searching for all this time was Prince Darian.

Man-whose-hand-I-threatened-to-slice-off Darian.

Soon-to-be-King-of-Aquara Darian.

I slumped into the nearest chair. This was not good. Very *not good.*

Naila took one look at my distress and laughed. It was a warm, affectionate laugh. "Oh, don't tell me you did not know."

My jaw hung slightly open in shock, and that was all the answer she needed. Naila's laughter echoed, growing louder.

"Princess Viriana was poisoned, and he had the nerve to try to stop me from treating her with salve," I said, trying to regain my composure. "He acted like he knew better than me."

Naila's chuckling abruptly stopped, and she tilted her head, a look of understanding in her eyes. "They always think they know better," she muttered with a wry smile, before adding, "especially the Royals."

I clenched my jaw, my irritation flaring again. "Yes, maybe it was Blotchbane, but I did the best I could."

"It was Blotchbane?" Naila's voice shifted, her tone now tinged with genuine curiosity. "How in the Sun Gods' names did you heal that? I rarely see Blotchbane poisoning cases."

"It was fine," I muttered quickly, hoping to deflect. "Some Silverworm, and that's all."

Naila stood and walked over to me. Her face was uncharacteristically serious. "You know as well as I do that Silverworm is only a painkiller. How did you manage to treat the poisoning? Are you sure Princess Viriana is completely healed?"

"Pretty sure." My voice was steady, but the unease gnawed at my insides.

"It's just... something like Blotchbane is really hard to heal. Even Aquara can't manage it with all their fancy medicines." Naila eyed me carefully, her brow furrowing. "How did you do it?"

I thought back to the light that had poured out of my hands during the treatment. It had been blinding, and I had tried to shield it with my body. I was not sure if anyone had noticed the glow, but it had been so intense that I could not have fully hidden it. When Princess Viriana's pale, smooth skin had returned to its natural color after I finished, it was *unsettling*. Almost magical.

"I—" I trailed off, trying to push the memory back. "I don't know. Maybe it's easier to heal the younger ones," I guessed.

"Solara, Prince Darian said you saved his sister's life."

A pool of blood flashed into my vision. Colorless lips. A faded pulse. A mountain of crimson-soaked gauze. The blinding light from my palms. Then, seconds later, an unblemished, perfectly smooth back with no trace of blisters.

I shivered.

I busied myself at my worktable, avoiding her stare. "It was just a poison that responded well to treatment. Who would have thought a Prince could be so overdramatic?"

Naila hovered around me for a moment. Her eyes kept trailing my arms, like she might peel back my skin to find some answer hidden beneath.

I shifted uncomfortably. "Did he say anything else? Anything about my mother?"

"There was another thing. He asked if I had known you as a child. I told him I had, of course. He asked if I knew your father."

I held my breath. Naila was one of the few people outside of my family who knew that I was not the blood child of the Commander. "What did you say?"

Naila gave me a grave, meaningful look. "I told him everyone knows Arin Hawkthorne, the great Ignios war hero."

"So you did not mention...?"

"No," she said firmly. "That's none of my concern." Finally, she returned to her desk and resumed her writing, as if there was simply nothing further to be said on the subject.

We worked in silence for a bit longer until I finally worked up the courage to say the words that had been hanging on my lips all day.

"Maybe I should start taking some of the work up at the Palace."

Naila raised an eyebrow. "What was that you said about insufferable monsters? Now you want to dote on them?"

I scrunched my nose. "There will be no doting, thank you very much. I only mean that I can help. You don't have to do it all yourself."

She hesitated. "You know how Liora felt about it. She would already be furious about this morning."

The heaviness I had felt on the floor of the Palace washroom settled back over me like a leaden cape. "It's time to accept that she might not come back."

"Don't say that."

"It's been six months. There's been no sign of her."

"You can't give up ho—"

"Don't, Naila. Please. Hope without reason is... it's cruel." I took a deep breath, willing the burning in my throat to fade. "I can't keep pretending like life is still normal. Like she's not..." My voice wobbled. "Like she's not gone."

Naila sniffled a bit, but remained quiet. "It's not that simple."

"What do you mean?"

"When your mother made that arrangement, she did not merely agree to serve for a few years. She—" Naila's mouth snapped closed.

I rose from my chair. "Tell me, Naila."

She winced, her pity hanging in the air like a cloying scent. "The bargain was for life, Solara. Your mother agreed to serve in whatever manner the Crown requests for the rest of her life."

"What do you mean, 'in whatever manner the Crown requests'?"

"I don't know the details… that was between your mother and the Royals. She only told me that she would keep working here as much as she could, but requests from the Crown would be her priority."

My knees felt weak. I leaned on the table, gripping the edge. "And if she breaks the agreement?"

Naila rubbed her hands over her face and exhaled deeply. "I swore to Liora I would never tell you this."

"Naila, if this affects us, I have to know. It's my job to protect Kian now."

She looked at me with genuine pain in her eyes. "If she doesn't fulfill her end of the bargain, then her life would be forfeited. She would be executed by the Crown."

The room began to spin. Suddenly the shadows were too bright, the silence too loud.

I fumbled for words. "But… the King—Kian says he's unconscious. If he dies… maybe no one else knows. Maybe—"

"Prince Darian knows. He's the one who negotiated it with your mother on behalf of the Crown."

When I returned home, the house was shrouded in silence. Kian and Father were already asleep, their rooms dark and still. The only sounds were the occasional creak of settling wood and the distant, rhythmic chirping of nocturnal insects. A small candle flickered in the center of the table, serving as the only source of light.

I tiptoed through the dimly lit doorway, careful not to disturb the peaceful slumber within. My fingers brushed against the worn surface of the small wooden cabinet by the entrance, its once-polished finish now dulled by years of use. In the top drawer awaited my favorite pastime, our collection of maps.

I retrieved my maps from an antique wooden chest. It was ornately carved with intricate patterns and symbols, a family heirloom passed down through generations. Each map was carefully rolled and tied with a leather string, its edges frayed and yellowed with age. I laid them out on my sturdy oak desk, cluttered with various tools of cartography: compasses, magnifying glasses and pencils of different grades.

The maps themselves were beautiful works of art. Delicate lines and swirls of ink depicted vast landscapes, mountains, volcanoes, and deserts. Some were adorned with detailed illustrations of mythical creatures and elaborate compass roses. The ridges and lines of the terrain were meticulously etched, each peak and valley brought to life through the cartographer's skillful hand.

Every year, the dunes shifted, rendering any attempt at accurate mapping a challenge. Yet, there was something profoundly stable and reliable about a map, even if it was just a representation of an ever-changing landscape.

My favorite was Haren. Ironic, because all of our maps featured bits of Haren, but this one captured the realm in its entirety. I traced over the belching buildings of the Technology District in the Upper East. Then, I passed over the central capital, Sand City, where I had spent most of my life. The Relic District in the south was the place of knowledge and the ancients. Towering libraries and devices that captured audible bits of history intrigued me the most. Apparently, you could listen to speeches from the Aquara Elder recorded a millennium ago.

After my recent visit to Aquara, I wondered what the Palace would look like on a map. How big were the silver spires compared to the rest of the map? I regretted that I had not paid more attention to our journey in the Sand Skimmer, too distracted by my talk with Eloisa. Aquara remained a mystery to me, its layout and secrets unknown. Determined to learn more, I rifled through my collection until I unearthed my mother's map buried beneath a pile of other charts. Mother had shared my love for maps, and I hoped to find some clue she might have left behind before she disappeared.

As I flipped through the fragile pages, a slip of paper fluttered out and landed softly on the floor. I picked it up. My pulse quickened when I recognized my mother's handwriting. At the top of the slip was a "To-Do" list, written in what looked like fresh ink from only a few weeks ago. My heart raced as I carefully unfolded the paper.

9

The Message

The scrap of parchment was no bigger than my hand. It had been tucked between two maps, so far down in the stack that I almost missed it. Not the kind of place you hide something if you want someone to find it, but not the kind of place you store it if you are planning to throw it away, either.

The handwriting was hers. I would recognise those curling tails on the y's anywhere.

I read the first line: *Tell D about the drying wells.*

D could mean a dozen different people, but only a few made sense. Daren from the archives, maybe, or Daria on the Aquara council? Drying wells. What were those?

Next: *Pack — herbs, maps, the silver vial.*

Herbs I understood. She never went anywhere without her healer's pouch, the one frayed along the drawstring from years of use. Maps made sense, too. She liked to claim she could wander anywhere, but I had seen her study charts until her eyes went red. The silver vial. My hand hesitated over the words. I had only seen it once, years ago, tucked into the back of her chest beneath folded linens. I had asked about it, and she had shut me down so quickly I almost missed the change in her tone.

On the line below: *Visit hidden library (use east tunnel).*

The hidden library had been one of those whispered-about places in my childhood, supposedly off-limits for typical Relics and containing books too old for the council's approval. I used to imagine it smelling of dust and river water, with shelves that creaked when you brushed past, but what was the "east tunnel"? From where?

Under it: *Emberberry — harvest before third moonrise.*

This one made no sense. I had enough Emberberry to last months, and she rarely asked for it at the Palace or the healer's center. It bloomed later in the season; the third moonrise was weeks early. Why else did she need it if not for the healer's center?

And then, below all of it, as if she had almost forgotten to write it: *Blotchbane.*

My breath caught. The name of the poison that had marked Princess Viriana's skin in raw, mottled patches. My stomach clenched. Had she been trying to obtain it for use ? The word was there, scrawled in her unmistakable handwriting, and at that instant, I felt the painful truth. I barely knew my mother.

I stared at the list until the words blurred, each item bleeding into the next until I could not tell if they were separate errands or all part of one plan. For years, my understanding of my mother had been built on what I had seen of her work: the way she eased a fever, or the way she spoke up when someone was wronged. With every new discovery, the shadowy meeting in Paradise Row and this note, that image was tilting into someone I did not fully recognize.

I folded the parchment, slid it deep into my pocket and turned toward the one person who might help me make sense of it. Rhea.

The path to her house was muscle memory by now. I slipped through twisting back alleys, past shuttered stalls and cracked cobblestones, avoiding the noisy main streets. I moved quickly, almost without thought, my mind replaying the words on that parchment over and over until they no longer sounded like words anymore.

Before I could lift my hand to knock, the door swung open. There stood Rhea, framed in the warm glow of the hearth behind her. She held out a cup of my favorite tea, steam curling upward in delicate spirals, as if she had been expecting me all along.

"Dearie! Come in, come in," she exclaimed.

I stopped on the threshold. "Rhea… how did you know I was coming?"

Her chuckle was soft, like wind brushing through dry leaves. "The wind whispers, child, and you have the look of someone who has a lot of worries to share."

Inside, everything was exactly where it had always been: the faded tapestries on the walls, the low table with two cushioned chairs and the incubator in the corner where a pea tendril now climbed higher than I remembered. She noticed my glance and smiled knowingly before sitting down.

I hesitated, then pulled the note from my pocket. "I need you to read this."

She hummed as she took it, her eyes scanning every curve of the handwriting. When she finally looked up, there was something unreadable in her expression.

"This is your mother's hand." She traced a line of ink with her fingertip. "She never told you about this?"

"She never told me anything like this."

Rhea leaned back, the parchment still in her hand. "Your mother was a woman of many layers, Solara. She kept her deepest truths sealed tight, even from those she loved most. This is intriguing."

"Intriguing?" My voice came out sharper than I intended. "Why would she hide this from me?"

"Perhaps to protect you, or perhaps she knew that some things are more dangerous spoken aloud than left unsaid."

I clenched my jaw. "I'm tired of secrets, Rhea. I need to know what this means."

Her eyes softened. "She was involved in things most people would not understand. She was not seeking power; your mother never cared for that, but she *was* searching for something. Something she never told me outright. Whatever it was, it mattered enough to risk everything. Including telling you."

I leaned forward. "What kind of 'something'?"

Rhea hesitated, then looked straight at me. "She spent more time at the Palace than you know. Not as a guest and not as a healer. At least, not only as a healer. She had ways of slipping into places she was not meant to be and hearing things she was not meant to hear. When she came back, she was different."

I stared at her, my pulse racing. "Different how?"

"Like someone carrying a wildfire they can't put out."

I swallowed hard. "Why didn't she ever tell me? If it was eating her alive, why keep me in the dark?"

Rhea gave a small, rueful smile. "You've got your mother's fire, Solara. Which means whether you like it or not, you're in this now."

"Fantastic," I muttered.

Her sigh was heavy, but her eyes were warm. "You're just like her, you know. Stubborn as a mule."

"I'll take that as a compliment," I said, letting the smirk win.

As I made my way home, the streets blurred past, but Rhea's words clung to me, twisting and turning like smoke in my mind. If my mother had not been after power, then what had driven her? Why keep me in the dark all these years? I tried to picture her with her head bent over her herbs, wearing the faint smile she wore when she thought no one was watching. The image twisted. How much of that woman had been real, and how much had just been a mask she wore for me? Did she know I would find this note someday? Was that her plan all along?

By the time I reached the doorstep of my home, my hands were trembling slightly as I unlocked the door. The familiar scent of home wrapped around me, grounding me for a moment, but even the warmth of the house could not stop the restless questions swirling in my mind.

I shut the door and began pacing across the room, my mind racing. My mother had always been cautious and meticulous, but this was something else. I glanced at the photograph of us on the mantle, her smile frozen in time, so full of life and light.

My fists clenched at my sides. All my life, I had trusted her implicitly, believed in the world she had built around us. Now everything felt like a sham. I wanted to scream and demand answers from the woman who could no longer give them.

Fight.

The jar of Emberberries sat quietly on the shelf, its bright contents glowing faintly even in the dim light of my room. It seemed so innocuous, just a simple jar with a simple berry, but I knew better. Whatever power my mother had been protecting, whatever secrets she had locked away inside herself, were all bound to this.

I forced myself to stand, my legs trembling beneath me as I approached the shelf.

Fight.

My hand moved before my mind caught up, fingers curling around the jar, the smooth glass cool against my skin. I felt my breath catch as I lifted it off the shelf, its weight far heavier than it should have been, as though the consequences of my next actions were already weighing down on me.

I glanced around my room, my gaze settling on the corner where a small fire crackled in the hearth. A place where the evidence of what I was about to do could remain hidden, at least for now. With a sudden, determined motion, I raised the jar above my head, hesitating just long enough to think of my mother's face, the secrets in her eyes.

Then, with all the force I could muster, I hurled the jar downward. It shattered with a sharp, deafening crash, shards of glass scattering across the floor like forgotten stars. The Emberberries burst free, their glow snuffed out as they splattered against the fire, hissing as the flames intensified.

I sank onto the edge of my bed with my head in my hands. A part of me was furious at my mother for keeping such a monumental secret and furious at myself for not seeing through her carefully constructed façade. Another part of me, the part that had always admired her strength and determination, felt something else. A flicker of fear. Fear of what I might uncover. Fear of the power my mother had held so close, and the danger it could bring to me.

Rhea's words echoed in my mind. *Whether you like it or not, you're in this now.*

10

The Second Visit

My second visit to the Royal Palace arrived sooner than I expected. Eloisa, on behalf of the Royal Family, had requested that I check in with Princess Viriana to see if she had fully healed. This time, my medical bag was meticulously packed, each salve and medicine carefully chosen to treat Blotchbane. I was prepared, more so than before, and it gave me a small, steadying sense of control.

The journey on the Sand Skimmer felt unusually quiet without Eloisa's effortless chatter. I leaned against the cool window, letting the gentle hum of the engine fill the silence and watched the landscape shift. The transition from Haren to Aquara was startling: dusty clay buildings slowly gave way to colorful houses with freshly painted façades, neatly trimmed porches and grand, ornate doorways. Flowers climbed trellises, spilling over balconies in bright bursts of color, and fountains glimmered in the sunlight, their waters dancing in perpetual motion.

Aquara's capital, Nereidia, thrived on excess. Every surface gleamed, every corner seemed deliberately curated, as though life itself had been polished. Its people were striking, though not in the raw, natural way of Haren citizens. Instead, each Aquara possessed an otherworldly perfection, a subtle blur of refinement that smoothed away even the tiniest flaw. Faces were impossibly symmetrical, skin flawless and luminous, hair catching the light in perfect waves or bouncing curls.

I could barely tear my eyes away from their chiseled features and impossibly long lashes.

Magnificent, lush gardens bloomed everywhere. In front of each house were unique arrangements of exotic flowers and meticulously sculpted hedges. Fountains dotted the courtyards, with water cascading in perfect harmony, their gentle splashes adding a serene soundtrack to the atmosphere.

The Sand Skimmer glided smoothly through the city, offering glimpses of Aquara's thriving market squares. The Aquara had a deep nostalgia for all things artisanal, especially handcrafted products passed down through generations. Stalls overflowed with fresh produce, aromatic spices, handwoven textiles and gleaming jewelry. The aroma of street food wafted through the air, tempting me with scents of grilled meats, sweet pastries and exotic fruits.

Merchants called out to passersby, showcasing their latest technological gadgets and traditional crafts side by side. One stall in particular caught my eye. A vendor demonstrated a palm-sized device that projected a three-dimensional image of a map, rotating and zooming in response to his gestures.

Nearby, a butcher had a mechanical arm that transformed into various tools with a flick of his wrist. One moment it was a hand, the next a set of pliers, then a small saw. The fluidity and precision of the transformations were mesmerizing. As we passed his market stall, our eyes locked. He grinned devilishly, catching my look of disbelief as I gawked at his arm.

After several minutes, the Skimmer hummed to a halt in front of the Royal Palace. I swung my legs over the edge and felt the gravel crunch under my boots with a satisfying thump.

Stepping through the grand doorway, my stomach twisted at the familiar sight of the defiant bronze creature perched above the entrance, its gleaming eyes watching like sentinels. Inside, the air smelled faintly of incense and polished stone. A woman in vibrant silks approached, her hair braided in an intricate cascade down her back. I recognized her immediately as one of the carers who had tended to Princess Viriana's every need after I had healed her.

"How is Princess Viriana?" I asked tightly.

She frowned slightly, looking ahead before answering. "She's doing well. Healed. Quite quickly, in fact."

"Good."

We made our way to the room. I took note of the space, decorated with overstuffed chairs, plush cushions, and silken drapes shimmering along a wall of arched openings. A bed, carved from polished burlwood, stood in the middle and seemed larger than I remembered. A frail Princess Viriana lay mostly shrouded under layers of coverlets.

I approached the bed, set down my medical bag and offered a warm smile. "Hello, Princess Viriana. Are you feeling better?"

"Yes, thanks to you," she answered softly.

"No complaints from her at all," Eloisa chimed in. "Either she's exceptionally brave, or it was thanks to that miracle you pulled off."

"Oh, it's all her," I replied. "Blotchbane is rare, found only in Haren. Its scarcity makes it difficult to harvest and even harder to preserve. Quite the feat that it ended up here."

I noticed their eyes widen with fascination, clearly unaccustomed to hearing such obscure details.

"Could you... give me your arm?" I asked gently. "I need to check the wounds and make sure they've fully healed."

Princess Viriana extended her slender arm cautiously, her skin pale and smooth, with only the faintest traces of the past infection still visible. I examined it carefully, applying a light salve with practiced precision.

Curiosity tugged at me. "Do you know how you may have ingested it?"

She hesitated, fingers curling around the edge of the blanket. "I... I drank some water from the bathroom tap. I was really thirsty and... I did not know it was bad."

I nodded, a little surprised that water from one of Aetherium's most advanced systems could cause illness. "It's not your fault, Princess. You did not know."

Her eyes flicked down. "I should have known better."

I placed a reassuring hand on her shoulder. "It's alright. Everyone makes mistakes. What matters now is that you're going to get better."

She nodded slowly, though the tension in her small frame lingered. To lighten the mood, I smiled and asked, "How about a story? Where I'm from, there's a beloved tale called *The Weaver and the Star*. Have you heard of it?"

Princess Viriana shook her head. "No... I've never heard of it. What's it about?"

I eased into the chair beside her, brushing a strand of hair behind my ear. "It's a story about courage," I said, my voice soft but steady. "A weaver, living in a quiet village much like any other, discovers a falling star caught in her loom. At first, she's terrified and afraid she might shatter it, but slowly, she learns how to handle it, how to let it shine without breaking it."

Princess Viriana's eyes widened with wonder. "And... what happens next?"

I smiled, letting a small laugh escape me. "She tries again and again, sometimes failing spectacularly. Each mistake teaches her something new, about the star and about herself. When she finally frees it, the village glows brighter than anyone could have imagined. The weaver learns something important, too. That courage is not never being afraid or never failing. It's daring to try, even when your hands shake and your heart races."

I looked at Princess Viriana and smiled. "You know, I think you're just as brave as that weaver, facing all of this with so much courage."

A faint smile touched her lips. "Do you really think so?"

"I know so," I said confidently.

Her attention shifted, and I followed her gaze to a small, crumpled piece of paper she fiddled with, fingers lingering over it as if debating whether to show me.

"It's... nothing," she said quickly, pulling it closer to her chest.

"May I see?" I asked gently, careful not to push.

She hesitated, eyes darting away, then after a slow breath, she slid the paper toward me. "Just... don't laugh," she murmured.

It was a paper butterfly. "It's beautiful," I said softly.

As I turned it over, twisting it this way and that, I noticed intricate lines and subtle shades of ink on its surface. Leaning closer, I could make out detailed markings. At first, they appeared to be random scribbles, but as I studied them further, it dawned on me: this was part of a map.

"Do you mind if I unfold it for a moment?" I asked.

She nodded, lips pressed into a thin line, still cautious.

I carefully unfolded the paper butterfly, smoothing out the creases. As the paper flattened, my breath caught in my throat. It was not just any map. It was an ancient map of Aetherium, covering all four regions. I had never seen anything like it before. The only maps familiar to me were of the well-charted territories of Haren.

My eyes traced eagerly over the unfamiliar topography, trying to memorize the names of places I had only heard of in stories.

To the west lay Haren, with the gleaming Technology District in the north, where towering spires of glass and steel dominated the skyline. In the south, the Sandy Relics stretched across the desert, an expanse of ancient ruins and shifting dunes.

Eastward lay the expansive territory of Aquara, marked by shimmering blue lines indicating its vast network of rivers and lakes. Nereidia, where the Royal Palace was located, was illustrated with intricate detail, its canals and waterways fanning out like the delicate veins of a leaf.

To the south sprawled Terra, a vast land of fertile fields and bountiful crops. The Emerald Plains were lush and green, dotted with symbols representing the numerous farming villages. At the heart of Terra was Verdantia, known for its grand harvest festivals and rich, earthy culture.

Farther south, Ignios rose with its fiery volcanoes and treacherous terrain. The map depicted the jagged peaks of the Flame Range, with red and orange hues indicating the flow of lava. Near the base of the mountains lay Pyre's End, the crucible where soldiers underwent their final tests, surrounded by a scorched, barren landscape.

I traced the lines of rivers, forests,and mountains, noting the names of cities and landmarks that had been mere whispers in Rhea's fantastical stories: the Whispering Woods of Terra, the Sunken Ruins of Aquara and the Blazing Gorge of Ignios.

"Where did you get this, Princess Viriana?" I asked, awe and curiosity blending in my voice.

She hesitated, biting her lower lip, her eyes flicking away for a moment before meeting mine again. "It… it's from my father's office," she admitted quietly, a cautious smile tugging at her lips. "But… you can't tell him. Pinky promise?" She extended her little finger, her gaze searching mine for reassurance.

I gently linked my pinky with hers. "I won't tell," I said softly.

And then it hit me—I was making a promise to an Aquara. Not just any Aquara, but a Royal. A few months ago, the thought would have seemed impossible. It was odd, too, not to feel Prince Darian's usual overprotectiveness. I had half-expected him to hover nearby, as he had the first time I visited the Palace. If he had been so curious about me, as he had shown when he asked Naila, where was he now?

A woman's voice interrupted my thoughts, politely but firmly urging me toward the door. I exchanged quick goodbyes with Eloisa and Princess Viriana, slung my medical bag over my shoulder, and followed my escort to the Palace entrance. The Sand Skimmer waited, its engine humming low and steady as we lifted off. Outside the windows, the golden dunes stretched endlessly, like a sea of sand reaching toward the sun.

11

The Father

I returned home that evening with a fire still burning in my veins. My father took one look at me as I stomped through the house and grabbed two dull sparring swords.

"Outside," he grunted, tossing one to me.

I did not bother arguing.

Though my father's aging body had put an end to his days on the battlefield, his mind had never really left. Retired and without an army to train, he had turned his children into his new battalion. Until I began working full-time as a healer, he would drag Kian and me outside every single night to pass down his knowledge.

How to fight, by hand and by blade. How to creep up and sneak away. How to spot an enemy's strengths as well as their weaknesses. When to stand our ground and when to flee.

We were Arin Hawkthorne's most cherished soldiers, and he trained us well.

By now, the routine was so familiar that neither of us had to say a word. A certain nostalgic comfort warmed my tight muscles as we fell into position in the open clearing. Lit only by the moon and streaks of golden lamplight emanating from the cottage windows, we began to move in a wide, slow circle.

He raised his sword high — too high — the blade wavering over his shoulder. Despite my foul mood, I cracked a smile. He was baiting me with poor form, trying to determine how badly my temper had clouded my mind.

Though I was quite tall for a Haren woman, I was still outsized by most male opponents, especially the unnaturally large and muscular Aquara. Father had taught me not to cower at the mismatched qualities but instead to see them as strengths.

Smaller means you're faster and harder to hit, he would say. *Weaker means you'll be underestimated, better able to catch them by surprise.*

It also meant I had to know my limits. Wasting my energy waving a heavy sword above my head to look menacing was one of them.

"Energy and blood are the two most important resources in a fight," I taunted, echoing the words he had so often taught me. "Choose wisely how you spend them both."

He grinned. "That's my girl."

Despite his praise, he took advantage of my decision to hold back, lunging forward to bring his sword down at my unprotected head. I moved left before spinning right, swinging my blade in a broad arc towards his ribcage. I nearly clipped him, but he deflected at the last second.

We both pulled away, panting from the burst of effort as we resumed circling.

"What happened today?" he asked.

My smile fell. "Injured children. Unfair world. You know, the usual."

"Must be more than the usual to have you this worked up."

This time, it was my turn to engage, forcing his weight onto one foot as he sidestepped a quick thrust. I swept his ankle with my leg, and he dropped to the ground in a smooth roll that brought him right back to his feet.

"You were watching my right foot the whole time," he scolded. "Don't let your anticipation give away your next move."

A novice mistake, one I had learned to stop doing years ago. The fact that he did not point it out directly suggested he was more worried than he let on.

"Tell me what's bothering you," he pressed.

"I'm fine."

Before he could argue, I swung my blade in a swift circle toward his shoulder. He deflected, using my momentum against me to push my blade to my weaker side. I twisted to counterattack, but he knew my habits too well, and his sword blocked mine, the harsh gong of metal on metal reverberating through my bones.

Though I stepped back to regroup, he would not allow it. He pressed forward aggressively, our limbs and bodies moving through motions as familiar to us as a loved one's voice in our ears.

I felt my temper rise with each clash of our blades, my movements turning increasingly sloppy. I knew better than to bring anger into combat, but I could not seem to stop it. Ever since giving up the Emberberry, my emotions had become an uncontrollable firestorm, threatening to scorch everything in its path.

The butt of his hilt came down on my wrist, carefully aimed to strike a sensitive nerve. Searing pain rocketed up my arm, and my fingers unclenched against my will. My blade thumped to the peaty soil.

"Tell me," he pressed again.

My resolve fractured.

"How did you stand it?" I snapped. "When you were in the army, how did you stomach serving the Aquara?"

It was a question I had never had the guts to ask him.

Others had. Most in Sand City considered him a hero, or at least a seasoned warrior deserving of respect, but a few had accused him of being a traitor to his kind. His calm temperament usually paid no mind to it, though the occasional heckler had earned a fist to the mouth, from him or from me.

His expression went icy. His eyes darted to my fallen weapon, then back to me, a wordless order. I scowled and snatched the sword from the ground.

"I did not serve them," he said as we resumed circling each other. "I served Aetherium. All of its people, the Haren and the Aquara."

"But you took their orders. You fought the rebels."

"And I fought Aquara at times as well. My vow was to protect Aetherium from any enemy it faced, no matter what blood ran through their veins. I would do it again, without question."

I paused and lowered my sword. "But who decides who's an enemy?"

"The Crown does."

"And what if the Crown is the real enemy?"

"Careful, Solara." His severe tone matched his features. "You speak of treason."

My eyes rolled. "Was it not treason to the people of Aetherium when they came in and took over our cities? When they contaminated our water and soil? And when they reduced our rations of pulp?"

He stabbed his blade into the ground, then folded his arms. "Where is this coming from? You never cared about such things before."

His words felt like a blow.

"Of course I cared," I shot back defensively, but the truth gnawed at me.

I had cared, but only in the ways that affected me. I had cared when I or the people I knew suffered, when the injustices inflicted by the Aquara were forced into my path, shattering my comfortable little bubble. Now, I was finally starting to peer beyond the bubble's edge at the reality waiting outside.

"These lessons I've taught you out here, about fighting and facing opponents..." He trailed off, gesturing with the blade in front of him. "Strength wins, Solara. Strength endures. The Aquara have strength on their side, and they always will. Ignoring that will only get you killed."

"So we should surrender and accept it? You did not raise me to do that."

"No, I did not, but what have I taught you about fighting an opponent who's much stronger than you are?"

I sighed. Years of his lessons flowed mechanically from my lips. "If you cannot be stronger, be smarter. Choose your battles and your enemies carefully. Know when to flee a fight to win a war."

"That's exactly right." He came closer and laid his hands on my shoulders. "Those lessons are as true off the battlefield as they are on it. Don't you ever forget that."

His dark umber eyes locked onto mine, concern hiding behind his gruff expression.

For all his bravery, I knew the reality of sending his children out into this wretched world terrified him. The sparring and the lessons and the memorable one-liners had been as much about managing his own dread as preparing us for the battles he could not fight by our side.

"What if I don't want to sit back and do nothing anymore?" I said. "What if I want to fight back?"

He cupped my face in his hands, his skin rough against my jaw. "I cannot tell you what to do with your life, my darling Solara. Whatever you choose, be smart. Above all, survive. Your life is far too precious to me to be wasted."

I sighed and kissed his cheek, the wiry hairs of his graying beard tickling my face. "Love you, Commander."

His shoulders shook with laughter. "Love you too, soldier."

We grabbed our sparring swords and headed back to the house, his arm draped around me, tugging me into his side. "I'm very proud of the woman you've become, Solara. Your mother, wherever she may be, is proud of you, too."

Though I could not speak through the burning lump in my throat, I offered up a silent prayer that he would not live to regret those words.

"It's been a while since you and Father sparred."

Kian and I were sprawled out in our beds in our tiny room, his face buried in his latest creation, while I lay on my back and stared blankly upward. We were both far too old to still be sharing a room, but Haren tradition dictated that a child only move out when they married, and there was little chance of that for either of us anytime soon.

"Not since before Mother's been gone," I agreed.

I felt his stare shift to me.

"Did you tell him about the Emberberry? Or the Aquara?"

"No."

"Are you going to?"

I did not answer.

I gazed in admiration at the whorls of light skipping over the ceiling from the candles burning on our bedside table.

I swallowed the lump in my throat. "Kian?"

"Yes?"

"You're being careful with Princess Viriana, right?"

"There's nothing to be careful about," he blurted out.

I turned my head to look at him. "I would not blame you if there was. She is very pretty."

His face turned a flaming crimson that said far too much. He shoved his head even deeper into his book. "It's not like that. We're just friends."

"Alright. If you say so."

"Every boy in the four realms would give up an arm to be with her. She can pick anyone she wants."

"I can imagine."

"And she's a Princess. The only Princess. They'll probably marry her off to some inbred cousin the moment she finishes school."

I bit down on my lip to suppress my smile. "Probably so."

He slammed his pencil down, his voice rising. "And she's an Aquara and I'm Haren. You know the rules. No dating, no marriage, no children."

He looked at me, and my wicked grin gave away my thoughts. He balled up a scrap of paper and bounced it off my forehead.

"Fine, fine," I relented, struggling to wipe the amusement from my face as I turned my attention back to the ceiling.

Perhaps what I said next made me a terrible sister, a bad influence, or recklessly naive, but it was worth it to see the light in his eyes when he spoke of her.

"You know I would support you, right?" I said softly. "Even if you were more than 'just friends.' Even if you stole her from her cousin-husband and ran off to Ignios to elope and have a dozen forbidden babies, I would still be the proudest aunt there ever was."

I meant it. I would stand by Kian's side, whatever choice he made. Even if he was rash and foolish and broke all the rules, because I knew he would do it for me, too. He always had.

"Be careful, alright?" I said. "No matter what happens, I'll have your back. Just... be careful."

He only nodded. We sat in the dim quiet, the rustle of his papers the only sound. But I knew my brother. His eyes may have been on the page, but his mind was miles away.

12

The Voice

My father's warnings still whispered through my thoughts the following day. I had expected him to tell me to accept the reality of the Aquara's harsh rule and to find other, smaller ways to make a difference. Perhaps, in some ways, he already had.

There was something else in his words that lingered. Somewhere buried in his lessons was a challenge. A calling.

I did not know whether it came from him or my own heart, but I felt it as surely as the autumn breeze that chilled the sweat on my neck.

I was not made to sit and do nothing. I was made to fight.

As I made house calls to my patients throughout Sand City, tending to broken limbs and persistent illnesses, the voice that had taken up residence inside me whispered back.

It heard the calling, too. Now it paced, a rumbling beast in a pen, waiting for me to find the courage—or the madness—to set it free.

My last call of the day took me to the outskirts of Paradise Row, to a stretch of alleys where prostitutes hovered in every doorway, offering their services to the lonely souls who staggered out of the nearby bars.

A blood-curdling shriek pierced the air.

I had heard enough screaming patients in my work to know the difference between a cry of fear and a howl of agonizing pain. This one was unmistakably both.

My head whipped back and forth in search, just as it rang out again to my left, followed by shouting and a child's wails. I pulled my dagger from its sheath and broke into a sprint.

"Please, don't—my child! My child!"

Another scream drew me closer and I skidded to a stop at the edge of the road. A woman cowered on the ground, arms outstretched to shield a small child who was clutching her waist, crying hysterically.

Across from them stood a wiry man, his shimmering black hair framing an expression carved with hate. He wore a fine jacket in a rich blue hue, its ivory buttons undone halfway, revealing a pale chest beneath.

The glow of his eyes cut through the darkness of the alley.

The piercing blue eyes of an Aquara.

He unsheathed his sword, aiming it at the woman and child.

My hand tightened around my dagger.

"Get out of the way," he growled at the woman. "I'll make it as quick and painless as I can."

"This is your child!" Her tone wobbled between begging and sobbing. "How could you be so cruel to your son?"

"That half-breed should never have been born," he spat. "This is your fault. You should have ended the pregnancy when it began. You hid it from me for four years, and now that boy's blood is on your hands."

She pleaded, tears falling from her cheeks. "Let me go to the King and beg for mercy. Or—or I can leave. I'll take him to Ignios, and you'll never hear from us again."

"I can't take that risk. My family has spent centuries building our position with the Royals. I will not have some Haren whore and her illegitimate spawn ruin everything we've worked for."

The venom that dripped from his voice seemed to infect his movements as he swung the sword back and forth in a show of menace.

The voice inside me roared to life.

Fight.

"Get out of the way, or I'll kill you both," he ordered.

"Like hell you will," I snapped, unsheathing my second dagger. "Step away from them."

He barely acknowledged me, waving his hand with disinterest. "Leave here, Haren scum. You want no part of this."

"Oh, but I do," I growled back.

A smarter, more rational part of my brain gripped my resolve and dug in its heels, hissing at me to heed the man's warning and walk away. This was not like the aggressive school bullies I was used to tangling with. This was an Aquara.

Smart and rational were privileges of the fortunate few who could afford to close their eyes to injustice and walk away.

My people of Sand City had never been granted such luck, and I was not built to walk away.

"Choose your battles and your enemies with care," my father had said.

Today, I chose this battle. Today, I chose this enemy. I would not let one more innocent child perish at the hands of the Aquara.

Fight.

I dropped my chin and marched toward him.

He drew up his sword, blocking my path. I swore, jerking back, my hand pausing in mid-air.

"This is my last warning," he barked at the mother.

She turned to me with watery eyes that had lost all hope. "Save my son," she pleaded. "Let me die but, I beg of you, save *him*."

I froze as recognition smashed into me. This was the woman who had helped me the day of my mother's disappearance, distracting the men chasing me so I could escape. She might very well have saved my life that day and now her fate was in my hands.

The man roared, swinging his arm forward, and the thud of blade against flesh rang out as her scream of agony burned through my head. The dark blade sank into her arm, blood splattering everywhere. The cut spread wider, her blood trickling in a slew of tiny waterfalls to the ground below.

I reached for my sword. In response, he unsheathed another blade and held it at my neck.

If I could not get through with words, my blades would. I cocked my arm and launched one of my twin daggers, carefully aiming at him.

My heart sang as my blade hit its mark. The point dimpled into the soft flesh of his shoulder, making the kind of wound that would leave a scar for a lifetime.

Buried deep beneath my fear, a cold numbness spread through me at the idea of his death at my hands. Not a sadness or regret, but a dark acceptance that made all my precious ideals seem distant and foreign.

As quickly as it came, despair took its place. The knife bounced harmlessly to the ground without leaving so much as a scratch.

My blades. My worthless, cheap, and Godsdamned Haren blades could not pierce Aquara skin. I might as well have tried to pelt him to death with a pebble. It had been such a pathetic attack, he had not even turned his head to acknowledge it.

I looked on in horror.

"Gods save me, please," the woman sobbed. A second blade flew through the air and plunged into her throat. Blood bloomed along her collarbone and trailed down her chest like a cruel necklace of dangling rubies.

My gaze locked on a pair of frightened blue eyes beneath her slumping body. The child was too young to understand what was happening, only that his mother was hurt, he was scared and he did not know what to do.

Neither did I. I could not get to him, could not save his mother and could not stop his father. I could swagger and act cocky, making my brash threats against the Aquara all day long, but in the end I was just another powerless Haren.

As I sank to my knees, I watched the man thrust his arm upward. The blade impaled the woman's body. He swung the blade to the side, and she flew across the alley and thudded against a thick stone wall.

I flinched at the sickening crack. I knew the sound of shattering bone when I heard it. When I finally mustered the courage to look, my gaze met the vacant, glassy eyes of a corpse that would see no more.

Fight, the voice demanded. Fight.

A snarl erupted from my chest. "You killed her, you disgusting monster!"

He did not hear me. His eyes were singularly focused on his next target.

I frantically gestured toward the boy. If I could get him to safety, then make just the right throw.

"Come to me," I coaxed.

His face shifted between me and his approaching father, his features pinched and unsure. He took a step toward me before pausing with a wary glance in my direction.

"I don't want to do this, but I don't have a choice." The man spoke low, though loud enough for me to hear, and I wondered which of us he was trying to convince. "I have to do it. It's the law."

"You don't have to," I pleaded. "I won't tell anyone. I'll take the child away and say he's mine."

He paused.

"If we are found out, I'll bear the consequences myself," I rushed out. "I don't know your name… I could not turn you in even if I wanted to. No one will ever know."

His gaze turned thoughtful as he stared silently at his son. His eyes rose to me, and my heart lurched to a stop.

"Please," I whispered. "He's just a child. Don't do this."

His face hardened. "No."

He closed his eyes as if cowardly hiding from the truth of what he did next. With a single outstretched hand, he swung his blade.

Fight.

Instantly, I moved. My father's blade left my hand and soared toward the Aquara. This knife was still new and foreign, its delicate balance so different from my heavy daggers. My years of training were enough to put the blade in his neck, but it struck too far from any veins that would bring him down.

He stumbled backward, hands fumbling at his throat as dark crimson spilled through his fingers.

In the midst of the chaos, I launched toward the boy and covered his body with my own. He was curled into a ball, his tiny arms wrapped protectively around his dirt-streaked knees.

"You bitch—you stabbed me!" The man's words came out gurgling and half-drowned in blood, but he managed to stay on his feet. The shock in his eyes twisted into something sharper and angrier.

He jerked the knife from his neck and let it rattle to the ground. I watched in horror as the gash began to clot before my eyes.

I knew they could heal, but to see it in action was astonishing. I watched the wound that would be fatal for a Haren man cause no more danger than a minor cut for an Aquara.

Father was right. The Harens did not stand a chance, at least not in a battle of strength. If we had any hope of surviving them, it would have to be a game of wits.

Fight.

A plan began to form. I filled my lungs with air and screamed a single word as loud as I could.

"Help!"

The man balked, his rage cooling to confusion. I screamed the word again and again. My throat was raw from the effort of casting my voice as far as it could carry.

He advanced slowly, his sword glinting in the dim light.

"You should have walked away," he warned. "You Harens have such pathetically short lives, yet you're all so quick to throw them away."

"Fire!" I shouted again. "Fire!"

Nothing happened. My confidence in my plan was waning..

Death stared me plainly in the face, its toothy grin enjoying the misery of my demise. I was going to die in this forgotten alley. Would anyone even bother to check my body? Or would I be yet another woman who disappeared on the streets of Sand City, following in my mother's footsteps in one final, horrible way?

FIGHT.

The Voice thrashed, no longer asking for release but demanding it, snarling to be unleashed and bring the world to ash.

I had nothing left to offer the boy nor myself. No weapons or magic, only the protection of my flesh to shield him from his father's vicious wrath.

I had never really been religious. I had never sought the guidance of The Old Gods, and aside from the occasional sacrilegious swear, I had certainly never invoked any of The Elders, knowing better than to expect any help from the very same beings who had fractured our world into four.

Still, if it could bring even a sliver of peace, or carry a crumb of favor from whatever being ruled over the afterlife for this boy and his mother… I had to at least try.

Sacred, ancient words flowed through me: the Prayer of Eternal Rest, a forbidden prayer from the ancient Haren religion.

"End be your time, a trade in kind, a life well lived for peace to find…"

As the prayer tumbled from my lips, the man's feet shuffled over the dusty stone. He sauntered closer, my words quickening with my racing heart.

"…Be not afraid, as shadows fade, all pain and woe shall be unmade…"

"A blasphemer," he sneered. "Good. I'll sleep easier knowing you have earned your death."

"..Now fate, well-sealed, shall be revealed, for those whose worthy souls shall yield…"

"The Gods can't help you now, girl."

I wrapped my arms tighter around the child and squeezed my eyes closed.

"…In love and calm, our holy psalm—"

Then he struck.

13

The Aquara

Tingling exploded through my body. That same icy heat I had felt at the Royal Palace now poured into every gash and wound, setting my skin ablaze with waves of frost and flame.

A bright flash illuminated my eyelids, followed by an ominous silence.

I waited to feel something. Pain, impact or whatever lightness of being people believed they ascend to when they died. There was nothing, only my own panting and the fading sensation that had consumed me moments ago.

"How?" he stammered. "How did you...?"

I cracked my eyes open.

Nothing had changed. The child was still huddled in my arms. His mother lay dead in a heap against the wall. The Aquara man stood over me, slack-jawed and stunned.

He had missed.

He missed.

He shook his head. "But... I hit you."

The glint of light against metal caught my eye. If I could just reach it, if I could have one more chance.

He followed my line of vision. Sensing my intention, he lunged forward, swinging his blade once more.

I locked up as the darkness surrounded me.

Another icy tingling.

Another blinding glow.

My eyes closed in reflex. When I reopened them, his sword was on the ground next to him.

He had missed. Again? I had seen the attack with my own eyes, the blade was on a direct trajectory to my thundering heart. There had been no chance it would not have hit me.

Yet.

Our eyes met in parallel stares of confusion, quickly interrupted by the sound of yelling and approaching footsteps.

My plan.

"Fire!" I yelled again, lurching upright. "Fire, over here!"

A crowd gathered at the edge of the alley, including several burly men carrying buckets that sloshed with water.

Years ago, I had tended to a woman in these alleys who had been stabbed by her lover's wife. The wounds had not killed her, but they had left her unable to walk. After hours of crying for help with no response, she realized that in Paradise Row, no one was brave or foolish enough to come to the aid of a total stranger. However, if she yelled "fire," everything changed. A fire in these closely packed streets could take out a swath of buildings in minutes. While the people here might not risk their lives for a stranger, they would do it when their own lives were at stake.

The people who stood before me now might never intervene to save me from this Aquara, but they could be an audience. That just might be enough.

He looked at the approaching crowd and swore.

I hurled myself toward my fallen knife. My fingers closed around the cold metal just as my shoulder skidded across the grit-covered ground. I twisted my body and swung the blade at his leg.

Instinct guided my hand toward his ankle. Thanks to my training as both a healer and a fighter, I knew a cut at just the right spot could sever the tendon and render him unable to walk, but a trapped Aquara who could not flee might decide to take out this entire crowd. I did not need the man disabled; I only needed him gone.

My aim shifted at the last second, and I flinched at the knock of metal striking bone. Hot blood splashed across my fingers as the knife slashed through his fortified skin.

The man roared in pain and jerked away. He yanked the dagger from his leg and hurled it in my direction, but it was more anger than aim, and the knife skittered harmlessly across the ground in front of me.

I grabbed it and glared up at him. "Go now, or I'll aim for your face next."

His nostrils flared. I saw, in the jerky movement of his eyes, that he was committing my face to memory, filing me away to deal with later. He gave a final glance at the boy, then fled across the opposite end of the alley.

Murmuring and grumbling arose from the crowd.

"What's going on?"

"Where's the fire?"

I scrambled to where the boy still lay curled into a tiny ball. "You're safe," I whispered, gently tugging at his arms. "No one's going to hurt you. He's gone."

His hand pulled away too easily. There was no strength in his grip, no resistance when I released his arm and watched it thump back to his side.

No.

I rolled the child onto his back. His clothing was punctured in too many places to count, his entire front covered in the dark, ruby stain of blood. His eyes were open and lifeless.

"No!" I screamed, reaching for his neck.

No pulse.

"Think, Solara," I hissed at myself. Force air back into his lungs, pound on his chest, jerk his heart back into rhythm, pack the wound with gauze and give him meadswart to speed the clotting. 'He had already lost too much blood."

It was too late.

I was too late.

I drew him into my arms and wept.

If I had come by sooner. If I had not hesitated to attack.

I dropped my forehead to his chest, silently begging his forgiveness for my failures as my tears mixed with the still-warm blood that pooled over his small body.

A hand grazed my arm. "I'm so sorry about your son," a voice said softly.

I could not stand to look away. I could barely force myself to breathe between my gasping sobs.

"He's not mine," I choked out. "His mother. She's over there, by the wall."

"May the Sun Goddess receive them. Did you know them?"

I shook my head, unable to speak.

An older man with thinning gray hair and a curling, peppered beard crouched at my side and touched the boy's ashen face.

"That foolish girl, getting wrapped up with one of them," he said, clicking his tongue. "She should have known better than to lay with the kind of creature that would kill its own young. What kind of life was he to have, with a death sentence hanging over his head for the rest of his days? Today might have been the first time he ever left his home."

My body quivered with rising fury, now so deeply woven into my devastation and guilt. It seemed that people, everyone around me, had lost all sense of right from wrong.

"He should not have to live like that," I yelled. "He did not choose to be born to that vile monster. These intermarriage laws are evil and wrong and that Godsdamned King—"

The man shushed me and glanced nervously over his shoulder, though the crowd had already grown bored and dispersed. Dead bodies were hardly an unusual sight in these parts.

"Hold your tongue, young woman. No sense getting yourself killed over a stranger."

"This boy was one of ours, too. Shouldn't we protect him? Shouldn't we fight back and make them pay?"

These were dangerous, deadly words. This man could make a pretty penny turning me in for treason. In a city of poverty, I might as well have signed my own death warrant.

With the child's corpse still warm in my arms, I could not bring myself to care. I could no longer hold back my words, no matter the consequences.

"They're the monsters. Why should we have to suffer for their pleasure? Why should any of us bend for their flaming w—"

The man jerked to his feet and shook his head. "You go and get yourself killed, then. I want no part of this."

"Wait—please. I... I need your help."

He turned away and strode down the street, leaving me with nothing but the echo of my anger and the weight of the child still in my arms.

14

The Meeting

Tarek secured a room that night at an inn above a local tavern, a place where we could finally steal some much-needed time together.

The tavern was alive with boisterous voices that rang out with laughter, debate and the occasional drinking song. In the middle of the room stood a roaring fireplace that filled the air with the scent of smoke and pine.

After ordering pints of ale, Tarek and I curled up at a small table near the fire. I did my best to smile and nod as he recounted the news he had heard from around the realms.

"...And that's how I decided to go to Ignios and ask them to turn me into a half-peacock, half-leopard, with wings that can shoot rainbow lasers!"

I blinked at Tarek a few times. "Wait—what?"

He smirked. "Ah, so you *were* listening."

My cheeks flushed, my lashes lowering. "I'm sorry. Long day."

"Anything you want to talk about?" He nudged my untouched plate and still-full pint in silent encouragement. "You've looked like a ghost all afternoon."

I took a long swig of my drink, stalling.

"Just my mother, that's all."

He reached across the table and brushed his fingers against mine. "Did anything happen?"

The truth clung to my lips, nearly spilling off my tongue. Instead, I shook my head and pushed my fork around my plate.

"Solara, whatever it is, I would never judge you."

The Sun Gods must have been looking out for me, because I was spared from responding by the arrival of a swaggering, thick-bearded man. His lean body cast a shadow over our plates as he sauntered up to our table.

"I heard Tarek was wandering around town with a gorgeous woman, but I was so sure it was a dirty lie that I bet my dagger on it. Looks like I'm about to be one blade poorer."

Tarek snorted as he gripped the man's forearm in greeting. "Good to see you, Cassian. Cassian, this is Solara Hawkthorne. Solara, meet Cassian Varrick."

The man appeared to be late into his late thirties and, despite the faint web of creases around his eyes and mouth, the brightness of his joy brought a youthful charm. His dark hair was closely cropped in the usual military style, and he wore a tunic embroidered with a four-leaved laurel wreath, one for each region, the standard-issue Aetherium Army uniform. Though the fabric's brown color marked him as a Haren tradesman, his skin was littered with scars and his arms and legs were trim and cut with muscles. The body of a soldier.

I offered a hand in greeting.

Cassian's lips twitched into a faint smile. "A firm handshake. I see you don't come unarmed," he said, nodding toward the daggers at my belt.

"I like to be thorough," I replied, letting my fingers brush over the weapons.

He gave a short nod. "A Hawkthorne, indeed."

My chin lifted in pride. I might not have been a Hawkthorne by birth, but I took upholding my father's respected name very seriously.

Tarek cleared his throat and motioned for Cassian to come sit beside us. Before I knew it, the two fell into a lively chat about mutual friends whose names I did not recognize. I let my mind wander as I focused on chewing the piece of pulp in my hand, but I noticed with discomfort the way Cassian shot me glances every time Tarek was not looking.

Eventually, the men's conversation slowed, and Cassian turned to face me. "So Arin is your father then?" I nodded, and his expression softened as if my answer had solved a great mystery. "And Liora is your mother?"

Cassian's comment took me by surprise. "You know my mother?"

Though my mother was highly regarded and well known among healer circles, she was relatively unknown otherwise. I motioned to his tradesman's tunic. "Are you a healer?"

"No, my trade is far less honorable than that of the noble healers." He smiled. "I'm a bladesmith. I made a weapon for your mother once."

My mother never went anywhere unarmed, a trait I had chalked up to my father's insistence but, unlike me, she was careful to always keep her weapons well concealed. I thought back over her collection of easily hidden blades and wondered which one had come from his hands.

"She's a hell of a woman, that Liora," he said. "I can see where you get it from."

Another flutter of pride danced through me, this time shadowed by the whisper of grief.

"When did you last see her?" I asked.

Before Cassian could respond, the table jolted as if struck. He and Tarek exchanged matching glares that had my brows rising, but Cassian rubbed his leg and quickly continued.

"We met in the army and we've stayed in touch since then." It was not the answer to my question, but a neat deflection. His focus moved to the sheaths at my hip. "I can make one for you, too, if you'd like. Something quick and stealthy to replace those giants you're hauling around." His voice dropped. "And sharp enough to pierce through thick Aquara hide without losing a limb."

I frowned at my twin daggers. I had stolen them from my father when I was twelve. As a child, I had been in awe of those daggers. They had served me well enough in the years since, even if they were a bit bulky at times.

"In fact, I've got something that would be perfect for you." He reached into his boot and pulled out a short blade. Its smooth metal was the color of a storm-darkened sky, the telltale sign of Igniosian steel, one of the only substances that could pierce Aquara skin. Its onyx handle was carved with wavering flames on one side and interwoven branches on the other. He balanced it between his fingers, running a thumb along its edge before sliding it across the table to me.

It was an exquisite weapon, the kind I would normally have to save for years to afford.

"I can't," I said, even as I ran a fingertip along the cool metal. "It's beautiful, but I can't possibly pay for it."

Cassian shrugged. "Take it." His tone left no room for argument. He unclipped the matching sheath from his boot and tossed it to me.

"You can't mean that. You could sell this for a small fortune."

"If I sold it for what it was worth, only the Aquara could afford it." His happy mask slipped for a split second, resentment creeping across his features. "I get enough of arming their kind during the day. Just promise me you'll watch this one's back." His smirk returned as he elbowed Tarek in the ribs.

Hesitantly, I dared to pick it up. Its weight was shockingly light despite its sturdy feel, yet well-balanced in my hand. My fingers grazed the etching along the hilt, noting how the deep grooves caught my skin and improved my grip. A clever design with as much function as form. The dull gray metal had been brushed to a matte finish, allowing it to be concealed more easily in the dark.

It was a weapon more suited for an assassin than a healer.

I reluctantly offered it back to him. "I really can't take this, it's far too generous."

He raised his hands, refusing to touch it. "Then pay me in a favor. One favor, to be chosen and called in at some later date."

"What favor?" Tarek cut in. He shot his friend a frown that suggested he knew exactly the kinds of favors Cassian usually traded in.

"Don't get your breeches twisted. Nothing scandalous. Unless the lady prefers scandal." His expression turned positively wolflike.

"The lady does not," I answered. "Nothing illegal. I'll agree to any other favor within my power to grant."

"And nothing dangerous," Tarek added.

Cassian shot him an exasperated look.

"If it's not dangerous, I understand it's not worth wasting a favor on," I said as I sheathed the dagger and secured it to my boot. I marveled at how it was almost undetectable against my calf.

Cassian roared with laughter. "Fenwick, you better hold on to this one." He slapped a very nervous-looking Tarek on the arm. "If you can."

I awoke to a cold, empty room.

I had left Tarek and Cassian in the tavern downstairs, happy to let them drink and banter while I enjoyed the solitude of a quiet room, but the more I lay in bed the more my mind flooded with demons nipping at my heels.

My missing mother. The agreement between her and Prince Darian. The cryptic notes. The Emberberry.

Each question was a stone slab in a wall surrounding me on all sides, thick and ivy-coated like the one I had seen encircling the Palace Gardens. My mind pushed back against the barrier, clawing for answers, but my fists only scraped and bled as the walls closed in tighter and tighter.

In retrospect, solitude might not have been such a good idea.

After only a few minutes, I had already tucked into the scratchy cotton sheets and succumbed to the refuge of sleep.

Now, I was wide awake. The empty expanse of bed beside me was cold and still neatly made. Tarek had not yet come back.

A peek through the window at the moon hanging low in the sky told me dawn was nearing. Worry crept up my spine, forcing me out of bed and back into my clothing and blades.

As I wandered through the dim hallway and down the stairs to the tavern, worn hardwood planks creaked under my footsteps, slicing through the heavy silence. The air was thick with the scent of stale ale and damp wood, but there was no lively chatter from patrons, no clinking of glasses or dishware.

A hiss of whispers lured me deeper into the dining room. Around the corner, a group of eight men crowded around a single, frail candle at the center casting ghoulish shadows along the oak-paneled walls. Their shoulders hunched forward, expressions excited but earnest as they murmured in low voices.

I breathed a sigh of relief when I spotted the dimpled jawline and disheveled hair of Tarek's profile seated beside Cassian. The grin that had earlier seemed permanently stamped on Cassian's face was gone, replaced by furrowed brows and a hand rubbing unhappily at his beard.

One of the men slammed his fist into the table, and I flattened against the wall. As emotions and voices grew hot, fleeting words and stunted phrases made their way through the room.

"...we cannot allow...."

"...send word to the others..."

"...gathering forces..."

"...almost time..."

"...war..."

The last word struck like a viper's fangs sinking into my skin.

War.

What war? Aetherium had been at peace for my entire lifetime. If there were threats from abroad, surely my father would have mentioned something.

Or perhaps, with my mother missing, he had kept any troubling news to himself to spare us further worry. Just as Kian and I had been keeping our problems from him, and each other.

Anxiety tightened around my neck.

Fight, the voice inside me echoed.

A tingling sensation coated my skin, and the world around me went dark as a hazy image shimmered in my mind's eye.

I was standing on a battlefield aflame with silvery fire, clad in armor of deepest black that concealed mud and gore. My bloodied hands held a great, gold-handled broadsword whose blade was veined with scrollwork that seemed almost illuminated from within. I swung the blade in slow, menacing circles that dared my enemy to approach. A shadowed figure stood nearby, and lifeless Aquara and Haren bodies lay in a broad ring at my feet, as if they had been thrown back by the force of a massive explosion. The soil beneath me was lush and moist with water. So much water. My face was undaunted. Sad but strong. Unbreakably strong.

I cursed myself again for destroying my Emberberry supply and leaving myself vulnerable to these delusions, but something about this vision was different. Unlike the vivid hallucinations of my childhood, which had felt lucid and entirely real, this seemed more like a glimpse into something vaguely possible. Not a reality that was, but a fate that could be.

The vision faded as quickly as it came, leaving behind an energy humming in my blood. Though I was once again empty-handed in a dark tavern, I could still feel the glossy metal of the sword in my grip, still smell the rotten scent of death wafting on an imagined breeze. That sensation of power was intoxicating in a way that left me wanting more.

My cheeks flushed as reality settled back in. I had no place on a battlefield. I was a healer, not a soldier. Even if I was equally adept with a blade or bow, my father had wanted better for me than to romanticize bloodshed.

War is no game, he had once scolded after catching me giggling as I waged mock warfare against Kian with rocks and wooden sticks. *War is death and misery and sacrifice. War is making choices that will haunt you for the rest of your days. You fight to protect, or to survive, but never for the joy of killing, no matter how brutal your enemy.*

If war truly was coming, there would be no glory in it.

I was about to return to the inn when my eye snagged on one of the men. He had propped his arm on the table with his dirt-mottled sleeve pushed to the elbow. On his forearm, stark against pale skin, was a drop of water encircled by a vine. The same tattoo I had seen on Tarek's shoulder.

My eyes raked across the other men. There it was again on a calf, protruding from the hem of cropped breeches. Another on a chest, edging out from an unbuttoned tunic. On the bicep of another, midnight ink was barely visible through a white linen sleeve. One more, hidden beneath tied-up hair.

Each of the men bore the symbol on their flesh, a permanent mark of some chain that connected them.

Tarek had lied to me. I had asked him directly about the tattoo's meaning and he had lied to me.

To honor The Old Gods, he had said.

Honor The Old Gods, my ass.

It was an ancient Haren sign of defiance. A symbol of rebellion. A mark that, if discovered by the Aquara authorities, could mean imprisonment or worse. Those who bore it were considered traitors, insurgents and enemies of the state. Entire families had been torn apart for a single trace of the vine-and-drop. The ink was a commitment, a declaration of allegiance to a cause the kingdom had long ago deemed punishable by death.

I gritted my teeth and stalked out of the shadows across the tavern. Chairs screeched as I shoved them out of my path. The men startled at the sound, several tugging at their sleeves and collars to conceal the tattoos they had so brazenly exposed moments earlier.

Tarek jumped to his feet. "Solara!"

His wince only stoked my irritation. Whatever he had been doing, he clearly had not wanted me to know about it.

"These are my friends." He gestured to the table. "Everyone, this is Solara, the girl I was telling you about."

The men offered a chorus of nods and grunts in greeting but studiously refused to meet my glare.

"I thought you'd be asleep," Tarek said.

"I woke up," I snapped. "A word, please."

The other men glanced at each other and at Tarek, the corners of their lips quivering with the effort not to laugh at the doom their friend had gotten himself stuck in. All except for Cassian, who was grinning outright.

I turned and marched back up the stairs to our room, spinning on Tarek as the door closed behind him.

"I'm sorry," he started, "I did not realize how late—"

"I don't mind that you were out late." Tarek flinched. "Who are they? Why do all of you have that tattoo?"

He opened his mouth and paused, hunting for an answer and failing, judging by his silence.

"'For the Old Gods' was it?" My glare was scathing. "I can't believe you lied to me."

"It was not a lie, exactly..." He scratched the back of his neck, still avoiding my eyes.

"Do you understand how much trouble you could get in if anyone saw that?"

"We're careful. We don't let anyone see them."

"Like you did not let me see them?"

He rubbed at his shoulder. "That's different. I was not trying to hide it from you. There's no Aquara anywhere near here."

"You can't be serious!" My voice was hoarse with the effort of not screaming at him. "By the Sun Goddess, Tarek, we're in Haren. The Aquara army painted this whole region red the last time a group of Harens gathered under that symbol."

His expression shifted, the lines of his face hardening in a way that made him seem older, more weathered. "I am well aware of that, Solara."

"Tell me what's going on." I crossed my arms, one brow raised expectantly.

His voice went quiet. "Like you've told me what's going on with you?"

A long silence passed between us.

My conscience scolded me—he was right. I had been pulling away from him for weeks and his secrets, whatever they were, surely paled in comparison to the turmoil I was so carefully concealing from him.

There was another voice. A louder voice.

Fight.

It was a creature of its own, this thing inside me. It was a lit match that wavered eternally above the pile of kindling that was my shredded soul.

Tarek rubbed his face. "I don't want to argue with you. It's safer if you don't know."

"I don't need you to protect me."

"Are you sure about that?" he retorted. "You haven't exactly been yourself lately."

Fight.

Words bubbled up in my mouth. Awful words. Unforgivable words. Words that would break us in irreparable ways. The thoughts raging through my head struck true fear into my heart, even as they grew louder and more insistent.

Fight.

My eyes squeezed closed.

Tarek watched me struggle. My quivering hands flexed and fisted, over and over.

The anger drained out of him. "Solara, I'm sorry." He stepped forward and reached for me. I stepped away, staggering backward. Tarek looked as if I had slapped him.

Fight.

"Leave me alone, Tarek."

He stared at me for a few seconds, heartbreak in his eyes, then turned and walked out of the room.

15

The Rebels

If anything was worse than fighting with Tarek, it was the awkward tension that came next.

After giving me some space, Tarek eventually returned to the room and collapsed onto the bed. Even as we packed our things the next morning and stepped back into the familiar bustle of Sand City, an uncomfortable silence clung to us. Every so often, his eyes would linger on me, his muscles straining as if he were fighting against an urge to speak, but he held his tongue and so did I.

We made our way back on foot through the streets until the thicket of buildings grew denser. The scent of oiled machinery filled my nostrils, and the burn of hot sand being kicked up by my sandals signaled that we were nearing home. Meanwhile, the thick silence lay heavy between us, punctured only by the thud of our footsteps.

I had always been a spitfire growing up, and I was proud of it. An unbreakable spirit in a world that so desperately wanted me to be small, subservient and quiet. That spark was no longer courage or innocent mischief. Now it had become something destructive. If I could not learn to control it soon, I feared it would destroy me or the people I loved most.

We were several hours into our painfully withdrawn trip when I finally breached the silence. "You were right."

His attention darted to me, and he looked as if he had never been more relieved to hear a sound in his life.

"I'm not sure about that," he said.

"No. You were right. Recently, I've just felt like I'm at a breaking point." My voice faltered, and I squeezed my eyes shut.

His leg nudged mine as he walked closer.

"It's not the worst thing to break a little now and then. It can rebuild character." Even without seeing him, I heard the teasing in his voice, his gentle peace offering. So I offered one in return.

"You're starting to sound like the Commander again."

"I'm choosing to take that as a compliment." When I opened my eyes, he was grinning. A weight lifted from my chest, not entirely, but enough that I felt a flush of joy.

"I'm sorry," I said. And I meant it.

"So am I." I knew he meant it, too. "I know you too well to try forcing you to talk about your feelings, but you know I'll be here if you need me, right? Always. No matter what."

My heart squeezed. All I could manage was a smile and a nod.

We continued without speaking for many long minutes. This time, it was Tarek who broke the silence.

"About a year ago, I watched an Aquara kill a Haren boy."

My eyes shot to his, but his gaze stayed fixed ahead.

"I was making a delivery in the Relics District. The boy could not have been more than fourteen, right out of school. He was crossing the road, but his arms were loaded with crates and he could not see..." He pulled in a shaky breath. "One of them was riding a giant horse, the biggest horse I've ever seen. I'll never forget it. White as snow, with a patch of black between its eyes and as tall as a house. Gold ribbon in its mane. It was going so fast. Too fast for a busy road like that."

He shuddered and my stomach lurched.

"It was an accident. I know that. Just an accident, but the Aquara..." His eyes blazed with remembered anger. "He barely even stopped. Gods, he was swearing at the boy for getting mud on his jeweled saddle. When he realized the boy was dead, he sat there in his gold and finery and stared at the corpse like it was nothing. Then he brushed the dust off his horse and rode away."

Tarek's fingers clenched around his tunic. His nails dug into his palms with enough fury to suggest he was imagining squeezing something else between his hands.

"I carried the boy's body to three different villages, but no one knew who he was. I buried him on our family's land to at least give him some dignity."

A chill rattled through me. "Tarek... I'm so sorry. That's... no one should have to suffer like that."

He clenched his jaw.

"I was so angry, Solara. It snapped something in me. Our whole lives the Aquara have trampled all over us, just like he did to that boy and they don't care. They leave us in the dirt as if our lives are worthless." His voice was rising, growing louder, more fervent. "So I decided if they could take a life from us, I could take one from them. I strapped on every weapon I could carry, went back to that street and waited. Every day for a week, I waited for the man to come back down that road and I knew that when he did, I was going to kill him. I did not care if I died in the process. I just wanted them to *see* us."

"Tarek," I breathed, sorrow heavy in my voice.

I had almost lost him, and I had not even known it. I had been off somewhere teasing Kian, or perhaps working at the center and all the while, Tarek had been a few miles away, resigning himself to certain death.

I fumbled for the right words to comfort him, to convince him I would never judge him for being so consumed with anger that everything else was cast aside and forgotten. But that would require admitting a secret of my own.

He winced and continued. "A Haren found me. He took one look at me and somehow saw the pain I was feeling. I told him what I was considering doing. He said I could die a meaningless death in one act of vengeance, or I could channel it into something bigger. Something that mattered. Something that would make a lot more of them pay than just that one man." He finally turned his gaze to me. His features softened into a more serene expression. "When I said the tattoo was to honor The Old Gods, I meant it. They were watching over me that day."

"Who was the man?" I asked.

He briefly scanned the road for listening ears. "I can't tell you his name. It's one of the rules. Never reveal the identity of any member, even to those we trust completely. It's a group for Harens who refuse to accept The Aquara as the rulers of Aetherium. We fight back in whatever ways we can. We call ourselves The Protectors."

My body locked up, my heart leaping to my throat. "But that's the name—"

"Of the rebels during The Great Divide," he finished with a nod. "The Aquara thought they had crushed it completely, but some of the rebels survived. They've been operating in secret ever since, gathering information and weapons. The hope is that someday we'll be strong enough to try again and win."

War. I had heard them whispering last night. I could barely catch my breath as new questions and fears tumbled through me.

"And when is 'someday'?" I asked.

"We can't afford to act too early and fail again, but many think The Blood Sun on Solis Day was a message that the time is coming soon. But only if..." He hesitated. "Only if we have more people on the inside."

"Is that why your father is working as the Palace Courier?"

"No." His features sharpened. "My father is not supportive of the rebel effort. Nor is he aware of my involvement." He shot me a meaningful look, a silent request.

"I won't say anything," I said quickly. "To him or anyone else."

He slowed down and paused to face me directly. "Join us, Solara. The access you'd have at the Palace as their healer would be invaluable. You could find out their weaknesses, how to get around their healing abilities, maybe even test different poisons by passing them off as medicinal."

"First of all, I'm not the Palace Healer. I've only gone a few times to heal a young girl poisoned with Blotchbane."

"But you've seen the Palace..." Tarek pressed.

"Yes."

"Exactly! That's the closest that anyone in our ranks has managed to get to the Royal Family." Tarek stammered, realizing his voice was too loud and lowering it.

A sick feeling twisted my gut. Healers took vows to save lives. To use my knowledge and the sacred trust of my patients to do them harm instead would be unthinkable. As horrible as the Aquara were, I was not sure I was ready to poison them and have that blood on my hands. My father had always warned me, *Power without restraint will get you killed, Solara. Keep your hands clean. There's always another way.*

Tarek seemed to notice my apprehension. "You could at least pass along any information you overhear. Military plans, movements of their armies, weapons they're developing."

As I gazed at the road ahead, it struck me that this might finally be my chance to choose my own future. My family, my tiny village, even my work as a healer—these were all paths laid out for me. Dangerous as it was to work against the Aquara, this was something I could choose for myself. Whatever the consequences, they would be mine and mine alone.

Surely, the Aquara, especially the Royal Family, would not be foolish enough to disclose useful information in my presence. However, if they slipped up and revealed something that would not harm my patients, but rather protect innocent Harens, perhaps it would be worth it.

The voice kept demanding that I fight. Maybe instead of fighting someone, what I needed was not someone to fight against, but something to fight for. I could channel the temper smoldering inside me and direct it somewhere it could help someone, instead of slowly burning me to ash. If Prince Darian or any other Aquara were responsible for my mother's disappearance, who better than The Protectors to help me find the truth?

But...

I had taken a vow—one so sacred it was the very foundation of a healer's training. A vow that, if broken, could see me banned forever. If I were caught, it would not only end my career, but it would stain every healer's name. If our patients lost their trust in us, they might stop calling for help altogether. Innocent people could die preventable deaths. Needless to say, The Protectors were wading into real rebellion, so death was bound to follow.

"I'll think about it," I said finally.

Tarek nodded as enthusiastically as if I had given my full-throated agreement. "You won't be alone. I'll be there. And—well, I can't tell you yet, but there are other members you know. Maybe we could even recruit Kian if we manage to convince him."

"Absolutely not." I cut in. "Leave Kian out of this, Tarek. He's too young. I don't want him involved."

"He's not a child, Solara, he's nearly a grown man. He might want to help."

"I don't care. I'll consider helping you, but only if you keep him out of it. Those are my terms."

"It should be his choice—"

"Promise me, Tarek."

A flicker of judgment crossed his features, but he lifted his palms in surrender. "Alright. I promise."

"And I'm not getting a tattoo, either. Unlike you and your friends, I have no desire to get skinned alive when the Aquara spot it."

"Fair enough." He scoured my body with a heated gaze. "I like your skin just the way it is."

I arched my brow. "Does your little club even take women as members? I didn't see any last night."

Tarek leaned in closer, lowering his voice."My little club is run by a woman."

"Really?" I straightened. "In Sand City?"

A silence stretched between us.

"Who is it? Do I know her?" I asked curiously.

"I can't say. No revealing anyone's identity, remember?"

My shoulders slumped. "Would I get to work with her?"

"I hope so," he said, his eyes softening with some inscrutable emotion. "She is a force to be reckoned with. Just like you."

As we walked down the empty street, Tarek lowered his voice almost to a whisper, glancing over his shoulder as if the shadows themselves might be listening. He spoke of missions he had carried out, mostly delivering messages among members within Haren or to cells in neighboring realms. He explained how he had been working to persuade his father to let him assist with Palace Courier duties so he could intercept royal communications; however, his father knew enough of Tarek's hatred of the Aquara and therefore refused him that chance.

I listened without comment, feeling a knot in my stomach tighten with each story. He was so proud and so certain of his path. I knew I should be more worried, perhaps try to convince him to turn away from an activity that could so easily get him killed, but it could not deny the pull of justice behind it. Maybe he needed a purpose as much as I did.

To be able to share it with each other, maybe that was what we needed to bring us back together and restore what we had been before my mother disappeared.

"There's something else I've been wanting to talk to you about." His voice had changed. "About us."

I stiffened. Had my thoughts been so obvious on my face?

He took a deep breath and reached across to take my hand in his clammy fingers. "I love you, Solara. The truth is, I've loved you my entire life."

My heart tripped over itself. We had never said those words to each other before.

He looked at me with expectation in his eyes and my mind became a whirlwind of thoughts.

Did I love him? Yes, of course I did. He was my dearest friend, as close to me as family. I was unsure if I loved him the same way he loved me. The sweep of his thumb against the back of my hand felt like sandpaper on my skin. I had to fight the urge to pull it free.

"I know we're still figuring this out," he said, gesturing between us, "but there's one thing I do know. You're my girl, Solara Hawkthorne.

You're the one I want to spend the rest of my life with. I was hoping you would do me the honor..."

My mouth went dry. "I care about you, too," I blurted out. "So, so much. With so many hard decisions in my life to make right now, I'm so happy that I can be with you and just relax. Without any pressure."

Shame weighed on my heart. I knew what he was about to say and what he was about to ask. Like a coward, I was running from it.

A shadow of disappointment darkened his eyes. He nodded as we set back on the path and continued our trek to Sand City. I avoided his stare the entire way home, but his words—and our future—consumed my thoughts.

16

The Sickness

Two weeks had passed since our trip to the tavern and, for the first time in a long time, I felt a glimmer of hope.

After a few more visits to the Royal Palace and growing used to the familiar faces of Eloisa and Princess Viriana, I had been offered a position as one of the Palace Healers. The role promised the chance to keep a careful eye on Prince Darian while also staying close to the work my mother had devoted her life to. Stepping in her footsteps made me feel closer to her than I had in months and maybe, just maybe, it would lead me to answers about the mysterious trips she had taken before she disappeared. From a practical standpoint, the role had its advantages. I could watch everything: the small, unconscious habits of the guards, the patterns in the comings and goings of the Court and the whispers of alliances that might otherwise escape notice. All of it could potentially serve Tarek's plans and The Protectors' cause, but even thinking of it that way churned my stomach.

In the days since, I had pored over my mother's records, familiarized myself with the small trove of potions and powders that were reserved for their treatment (none of which, to my dismay, included Emberberry), and spent several long evenings being tutored by Naila on the nuances of treating these genetically superior beings that I had been so carefully segregated from all these years.

There was one substance I had learned could be deadly to the Aquara: Ashvine, a rare and venomous plant that thrived in the volcanic ridges of Ignios. Crafted into a blade, a single precise strike could kill instantly and even a graze wound carried the risk of infection from its searing, corrosive toxin. Despite their superior genes and accelerated healing, Aquara could not withstand Ashvine's effects. The poison worked deep in the bloodstream, shutting down vital systems with excruciating pain, and no antidote was known to reverse it.

It was one piece of knowledge that lingered in my thoughts for days afterward. This was precisely the kind of information Tarek's rebel group would want to know if I decided to work with them.

So, armed with an arsenal of newly acquired wisdom, I was ready to go to the Royal Palace. This trip would be the final follow-up for Princess Viriana.

The journey to the Palace on the Sand Skimmer had become almost familiar, with each cobblestone and archway greeting me like an old acquaintance. Banners fluttered from the towers above, whispering of the Palace's history, and the faint scent of polished stone and blooming courtyard gardens filled the air. It was then I noticed Eloisa striding toward me across the garden, her skirts swishing with the confidence of someone who already knew every corner of this place. Her eyes lit up like lanterns when they found mine.

"Solara! What a relief to see you again," she exclaimed, her voice bubbling with its usual brightness. "We've been waiting for your start here."

I matched her smile. "Eloisa, it's good to see you."

"I hear you're a Palace Healer now. Is that right?" she asked, her words tumbling out in a rush, as if she could hardly contain them.

"Indeed."

Without hesitation, she hooked her arm through mine and guided me toward a narrow side door. "There are more safety precautions now that you'll be working here. They're tiresome, really. You'll see. Just keep calm and don't let the guards' tempers rattle you." She said it with a flippant wave of her hand, but the quick glance she shot at me betrayed a hint of unease.

"No worries," I said evenly. "How is Princess Viriana?"

The sparkle in her expression faltered. "This visit isn't for Vira," she admitted, her voice dropping. "We have a bit of an unusual situation.

Vira and Prince Darian are in the King's Quarters. King Thalor is—" she hesitated, choosing her words carefully, "—quite unwell."

I raised an eyebrow, though I kept my tone calm. Eloisa pressed on quickly. "Prince Darian granted you entry himself. They're waiting for you. He wants you to examine the King."

A jittery thrill hummed through me. I was about to step within the same walls as the King himself and, more than that, my judgment, my knowledge and my hands were being trusted. Even Tarek's father, who had served as Palace Courier for years, had never been granted such close access.

The side door opened into the Palace's entrance, a cavernous stone chamber that swallowed us in echoing silence. Before we could take three steps inside, steel flashed in front of us.

Sword-wielding guards suddenly bombarded me with questions and made no attempt to hide their disdain. They demanded my name, qualifications, the contents of my bag and the nature of my duties in the Palace today.

After yielding to their enquiries, the guards eventually grunted their approval and tossed my bag back at my feet. Eloisa helped me gather up my scattered belongings and we turned toward the cavernous, marble-coated foyer when an armored forearm swung into my chest and stopped me short.

The man's eyes flicked to my daggers. "Members of staff must surrender their weapons before entering."

My jaw tightened.

"I'll need them for my duties here," I explained.

He retorted. "None of your duties here should require a blade."

I hesitated. "The last time I was here, I used this blade to save Princess Viriana's life. I need to cut bandages cleanly and stitch wounds, when the situation calls for it."

We held each other's gaze, neither one of us ready to relent.

"Solara," Eloisa said quietly, a plea and a warning.

"Get Prince Darian," one of the guards commanded.

Eloisa waved a hand frantically. "No, no—that won't be necessary. She'll leave them here. Right, Solara?"

The guard looked at me. "That's exactly what she'll do." One hand shot out, gripping my shoulder with a force that made my teeth clench. Who did he think he was? After everything, after saving their precious Princess, they treated me like a criminal.

A flicker of anger ignited inside me. My control snapped and I shoved the guard back with every ounce of strength I had.

The sharp clang of metal rang out around me as swords slid free from their scabbards. In an instant, I was surrounded by razor-sharp blades glinting in the dim light, each one aimed straight at my chest.

"Stand down."

The low voice reverberated against the stone walls.

Collectively, our eyes climbed up the twin winding staircases to the imposing figure atop the landing. Tailored black breeches, a jacket of deepest midnight blue edged with silver beading, a jeweled sword and ebony hair tightly bound.

Prince Darian.

"These women are here in the service of the Crown and the Crown has a right to maintain security measures for the safety of all on site," Prince Darian said coldly. "Is this how we treat His Majesty's civil servants? Solara, is this how you react to someone else's safety protocol?"

"But he was—" I began.

"But she was—" the guard interjected defensively.

Prince Darian stepped forward, his presence commanding.

"That will be all. You may go," he said to the guard, his tone leaving no room for argument. "I'll take it from here."

He turned to me, his gaze sharp and unwavering. "Miss Hawkthorne, you may keep your weapons as long as I am present. Dare to harm anyone in the Palace, and your access will be forfeited. Do we understand each other?"

I swallowed. "We do."

"Please follow me." He spun on his heel and strode toward the Palace interior.

We continued up one arm of the magnificent staircase and down a series of winding halls, each more decorated than the last. Intricate tapestries of the most vibrant colors, lace-like carved marble, glittering ceilings that glowed from within and everything bejeweled and gilded. Even the air smelled lavish, scented with the delicate sweetness of fresh-blooming roses. I struggled not to gawk at the splendor of it all.

"I understand you wish to join the ranks of Palace Healers, Miss Hawkthorne," Prince Darian said as we walked.

I nodded. "I'm hoping to help with my mother's duties in her absence."

"*All* of them?"

My eyes snapped to him so quickly it took my mind a moment to catch up. There was a weight to his words, an implication that prickled my instincts. His expression gave away nothing, but I sensed I was on more dangerous ground than I fully understood. I did not respond.

Your mother agreed to serve the Crown in whatever manner the Crown requests, Naila had said.

On the way to the King's Quarters, we passed two women in the hall with their heads bent close together, voices lilting with muffled laughter. They reminded me of magpies, preening and pecking at scraps of gossip. They each wore gowns befitting a grand affair, made from shimmering fabric and hanging stiffly over layers of puffy, candy-colored petticoats. Chunky gemstones circled their necks and wrists, and their unnaturally-colored hair was piled atop their heads with a mess of ribbons and colorful feathers.

"Cousins," Prince Darian greeted with a shallow nod.

"Your Highness," they said in unison as they rose and curtsied.

One of them, an elegant woman dripping in emeralds and mauve taffeta, fluttered her lashes in his direction. "How kind of you to come join us, Darian," she cooed with a coy smile.

"Prince Darian," he corrected smoothly. The woman's face burned pink enough to match her dress. "I'm here to escort the healer."

"Who is she?" the second woman asked. She was a good deal older but still quite beautiful, her dark violet bouffant streaked gray at her temples. Her features seemed carved into a permanent frown as she looked me over.

"This is the healer who treated Princess Viriana the day of the incident," Prince Darian said. He turned to me.

"Why does this one have weapons?" the elder cousin cut in, her words sharp enough to draw blood. She gestured at me with a limp, jeweled hand, her lip curling. "Imagine, parading about with daggers in the King's halls. What would father say if he saw?"

Her companion giggled, hiding her mouth behind painted fingers. "Perhaps she thinks herself a knight," she whispered, though not nearly quietly enough.

The elder woman's gaze flicked up to my face, narrowing like a blade being honed.

"I permitted her weapons while under my escort. She saved Princess Viriana's life," he reminded them calmly.

One of the women turned toward me with a half-smile that did not reach her eyes. "Oh yes, the poisoning. Tell me, is poor Princess Vira all better now?"

I forced a small smile, trying to keep it light. "It was touch and go, but I believe she'll recover."

Her delicate features twisted into a sharp glare. "A threat to a child's life is hardly a joke."

"Of course. I meant no disrespect." I kept my voice calm, though inside I was bristling. She crossed her arms, a thin smile twisting her lips. "I shouldn't be surprised that a suffering child is what you people find entertaining."

Her companion let out a laugh disguised as a cough. "Well, they say the Harens are hard people. Death must be dinner conversation where you're from." She gave me a sweet, poisonous smile. "How… rustic."

I ignored their comments and tried to answer calmly.

My abilities had been challenged, again. These women accused me of laughing over death, yet they had not seen suffering for a single day in their lives. Every week I treated children dying of thirst because their families could not afford water rations. I dreaded the winters when the homeless orphans were found frozen in the night. Meanwhile, they were here, walking through a Palace dripping with gold and jewels, enough wealth to solve every one of those problems, and they had the audacity to lecture me about poor, dying children. I clenched my fists silently, letting the anger simmer beneath my calm exterior.

Prince Darian must have sensed the tension, because he cut in smoothly, "If you'll excuse us," and inclined his head with a polite nod that brooked no argument. He gestured for us to continue down the corridor.

We had barely gone a dozen steps when a scoff rang out behind us, sharp and deliberate. One of the women spoke just loudly enough to carry, "It's hardly our fault those Harens can't take care of themselves."

My control snapped, and I was already half-turned, ready to unleash the words burning in my throat, when Eloisa's elbow jabbed hard into my ribs. It was a silent warning to hold my tongue. I forced myself to face forward, my gaze snapping to Prince Darian. His jaw ticked and I knew then that he had heard every word.

He slowed to walk beside me, his voice almost solemn. "Please accept my apologies. My family can be difficult, sometimes."

We continued through the Palace, moving past towering bookshelves in a library that dwarfed even the largest in the Relic District, their spines rich with colors and gilded lettering. We passed multiple lavish resting rooms, each adorned with silks, tapestries and velvet-covered chaise lounges. Prince Darian strode ahead with confident, long steps, while Eloisa and I followed closely, flanked by two guards. One wrong turn and the serpentine Palace corridors could easily swallow a visitor in an endless maze of rooms and hallways.

"I came looking for you in Sand City," he said suddenly. "I wanted to thank you for what you did for my sister."

"Yes, my cousin mentioned it. You're kind, Prince Darian, but truly, I was merely doing my duty as a healer," I said with a polite smile.

"Please, just call me Darian, if you don't mind," he replied before continuing. "I also wanted to apologize for my own behavior the last time you were here."

A silence stretched between us, broken only by our echoing footsteps. His brows dipped low. "Liora was supposed to tell me," he added, and my mind snapped back to memories of my mother.

"What?" I asked, my voice tighter than I intended.

"If conditions were this bad in Sand City, your mother was supposed to warn me so I could provide assistance."

A shadow passed over my expression. "Well… she hasn't been around to do that," I said quietly. His posture stiffened, a vein pulsing along his neck. "Besides, things are always that bad in Sand City. They always have been."

"If there is a family in need, tell me and I will make arrangements—"

"Respectfully, Darian, every family in Haren is in need," I said with defiant honesty. The words struck him with a weight that made him pause mid-step; perhaps no one had spoken so bluntly to him before. He settled his posture and looked down.

We finally came to a stop in front of a large wooden cabinet, flanked by guards: the King's Quarters. Its doors were intricately carved with images of flowing rivers and ancient battles. Darian opened it to reveal a room with a canopied bed, carved from polished, swirling burlwood. A frail figure lay mostly shrouded beneath layers of pristine sheets. Darian paused in the doorway, kneeling and dipping his head in respect, his voice dropping to a whisper.

King Thalor.

I had never actually seen him before. The King had come to Sand City on occasion, primarily to inaugurate one of the edifices of the Sun Goddess, sometimes placed around Sand City as a subtle threat against any surviving worship of The Old Gods, but my mother had been careful to keep me at home on such occasions.

I felt a hard yank on my arm. Eloisa was bowing low and shooting me an insistent look.

Right.

I sank obediently to one knee, though I could not tear my eyes from the King's face. I arched my neck, straining to get a better look.

He looked startlingly young and not nearly elderly enough to be fading away from what seemed to be the Aquara equivalent of natural causes. If he were a Haren, I would have imagined him to be the same age as my father.

I knew better. His reign had begun decades ago. What must it be like to have superior genes, better access to water and to outlive generations of Harens, watching them age and die, over and over? The idea struck me as terribly sad. Of course, these Aquara likely had never met a Haren they cared enough about to mourn.

I felt Darian's gaze settle on me. He had risen and was now standing beside the King's bed, tracking my every move.

Beside me, Eloisa held still. Her shoulders hunched in submission with her eyes fixed on the floor, waiting for the Prince's permission to rise.

"You may attend to your duties," he said.

I rose at once, gathering my satchel. From it, I laid out tinctures, poultices, rolls of linen and small jars of dried herbs onto a nearby side table. Then I approached the bed, my hands steady though my heart thrummed.

The King's eyes were closed. His breathing was shallow but regular. If Eloisa had not warned me of his months-long unconsciousness, I might have thought him merely sleeping. The hollowness of his cheeks, the sharp outline of bone under fragile skin and the stiffness of his joints told another story. His body was failing.

Despite my best efforts to detest the man, I felt a stab of sympathy. My head understood that he was responsible for countless atrocities, having reigned over generations of oppression and cruelty toward my people, but in this moment, my heart saw only a man on the brink of death.

"Eloisa," I murmured, and she hurried forward. At my instruction, she smoothed salve over the sores on his back and limbs, working it gently into the parchment-thin skin. Meanwhile, I pried open his lips to drip in a measure of Willowroot tincture to ease inflammation, then felt at his wrists and ankles, noting the swelling. I massaged the stiff joints in slow, practiced motions, then prepared a cloth steeped in Feverfew to lay across his brow.

When I stepped back, wiping my hands on a cloth, Darian's gaze was waiting for me.

"He is stable, for now," I said. "But he will need to continue using the ointments to alleviate his suffering."

Darian inclined his head, his expression grave but unreadable. "Understood. Thank you."

I gathered my satchel and nodded to Eloisa. Together, we followed Darian out of the chamber, the door closing behind us with a muffled click. The air in the corridor felt cooler, freer, though the weight of what I had just witnessed lingered in my chest.

"Solara!" Vira's bright voice rang out as she hurried toward me, her hands clasped in excitement. Her warm smile felt almost out of place after the heavy silence of the sickroom. "I'm so glad you're here! You'll be staying in the Palace now, won't you?"

"Yes," I said, adjusting the strap of my bag. "It seems I'll be serving as a Palace Healer for some time."

"Wonderful!" She beamed, almost glowing. "You'll have to let me show you everything. There's so much to see. You'll love it."

As she tugged gently at my sleeve, Darian's voice halted us. He was standing just outside the chamber door, arms folded, watching with that same piercing steadiness.

"Vira, you may show Solara the way to the Royal Apothecary if you'd like," he said. "But if you're not back within the half hour, I'll send guards to find you."

Vira rolled her eyes with a playful sigh. "He's always like this," she whispered to me with a conspiratorial grin. "But don't worry, we won't get lost."

As she slipped her arm through mine and led me down the corridor, I caught myself studying her face in the lamplight. The curve of her cheek, the tilt of her brow and even the spark in her eyes. It was Darian's face reflected back in softer lines. Though his manner was guarded and hers open, the bloodtie between them was unmistakable.

Vira's cheerful tug pulled me from the thought. "Come on," she said. "I'll show you the Nurse's Quad!"

17

The Emberberry

A few minutes later, I was wandering the Palace Apothecary in awe, marveling at shelves stacked high with glass jars holding every item one could imagine. Princess Vira had not been joking: medicinal supplies from every corner of the four realms filled the space.

Each shelf was lined with polished wooden racks, cradling glass bottles of every shape and size. Some were tall, filled with vibrant liquids that glowed in the dim light, swirling as if alive. Others were squat and round, holding powders in hues from emerald green from crushed mountain herbs, deep crimson from the petals of a flower that only bloomed once a century, and ghostly white from the roots of a plant rumored to grow in the shadow of death itself.

Bundles of dried herbs hung from the ceiling, their sharp, sweet and earthy scents mingling in the air. There were leaves as wide as a man's hand, dark and leathery, alongside delicate fronds that shimmered with an iridescent sheen. Some plants were encased in crystal boxes, too poisonous to be exposed to air, their tendrils pressing against the glass as though seeking escape.

A small chest in the corner displayed several vials filled with a thick, golden liquid: honey from the enchanted bees of the northern forests, said to cure ailments of the heart and soul. Next to it was a bowl brimming with translucent blue stones that hummed with a faint energy, a rare mineral said to enhance the potency of any potion it was mixed with.

I glanced back at Princess Vira. "This is incredible."

"Our people have spent years gathering all the things we need. Now that you're a Palace Healer, Darian will probably let you use this room whenever you need."

Just as I was about to thank her, my eyes snagged on a metal cage hidden in a corner behind a series of bookshelves. It was not the cage that struck me, but the vibrant color blaring through it. I inched closer. Could it be?

My breath caught.

Even if the violent crimson hue had not given the Emberberry away, the distinctive crescent-shaped vial was so familiar to my palm that I could pick it out blind. I had held it in my hand, glared at it with trepidation and resentment, nearly every day that I could remember.

It was the one medicine I could not make, buy or substitute. With my own supply sitting shattered in our fireplace, I had done my best to convince myself I did not need it anymore.

No matter how much I tried to dismiss it, I knew my symptoms were returning. The same symptoms that had haunted me all those years ago, visions and feelings that made me believe that I was doing things I should not be able to do.

Magic.

I had hallucinated that I had magic. I had been hysterical at the time, trembling at the horrifying prospect that I might be one of the monsters from the ghastly stories my friends swapped at school.

My mother had held me close, calmed me with soothing words and a tender touch, and had broken the news that the man who fathered me had suffered from similar delusions that had driven him to his end.

"I had hoped it wouldn't pass to you," she had told me in a voice soaked with despair. "But don't you worry, my little warrior. I'll protect you. I won't let you end up like him."

As soon as I had begun the morning Emberberry regimen, the visions had stopped. Though it turned my mind cloudy and my emotions stunted, my life had returned to blissful normalcy.

Something intriguing caught my attention in the apothecary. I noted a heavy iron padlock secured to the door of the cage. "Could I get some of this as well?" I called out, motioning to the vials.

Vira followed where I was pointing with wide eyes. She looked around for spying eyes and ears. "Why do you need that?"

"I might need it," I said hesitantly. "Is there a problem?"

She shook her head quickly, curls bouncing. "Oh, no problem… It's just that I don't know much about them. Darian has someone bring a little every month and he always locks it up. He says it's really hard to get, something about the Crowns needing to agree first. I never asked why, it all sounds very boring," she said, wrinkling her nose playfully.

I gave a small, practiced smile. "I'll have to check my notes, then."

Her face lit up with sudden excitement. "Notes? You keep proper notes? You must show me sometime! I'd find them fascinating. I'm dreadful at keeping track of anything, half the time I can't even remember where I've left my shoes!"

My thoughts snagged on her words, my expression slipping before I caught myself. Vira, oblivious, leaned against the table and studied the cage as though it were a locked toy chest. "I don't even think the Chief Healer is allowed to touch them. Uncle Thalor lets Darian open it, but that's all. You must have been terribly clever to find some on your own." Her tone was pure admiration.

My pulse quickened. "I must be mistaken," I said quickly. "It must be something else. I was just… confused."

"Oh." She tilted her head. "Well, if you remember, will you promise to tell me? I'd love to know more about what you use for healing."

I hesitated, then risked a gentle prod. "Do you happen to know why they're so regulated?"

Vira blinked, lips parting in a small 'O' before curving into a helpless laugh. "Oh, I've no idea. Darian always says they're rare and important, but he never explains further. I think he enjoys sounding mysterious." She leaned in and lowered her voice like a gossiping sister. "Personally, I don't see the harm in them. They look like ordinary berries to me."

She straightened again, her smile bright as sunlight. "Anyway, I'm glad you'll be around more. The Palace can be dreadfully dull without someone interesting to talk to."

18

The Protectors

That afternoon I returned to a quiet house, my mind still reeling from the day's events. Not only had I met the one and only King Thalor, but I had also toured the Royal Apothecary, staring at row upon row of bottles and vials, cataloging the medicines in my mind.

The medicine I had seen in that cage was Emberberry. *My* Emberberry. I was certain of that. The bottle, its consistency and its color were too distinct to be a coincidence.

Why would a medicine be guarded so fiercely by the Crowns of Aetherium? How in all the realms had my mother managed to procure bottle after bottle of it? I had no time to linger on the questions.

I pulled my front door shut behind me, the click of the latch echoing louder than usual in the quiet street. My fingers itched to check the apothecary notes in my satchel, to make sense of everything I had just seen, but my afternoon shift at the healers' center would not wait.

Before I could even walk two steps, hurried footsteps pounded behind me. Tarek came jogging up, breathless and grinning. "So the Royal Palace, huh? What happened? Did you find anything useful?"

I shrugged, keeping my tone casual. "Yeah... I mean, it was the Palace. There was the King, the Royal Apothecary and a few other rooms."

"You... *met the King*?!"

"We're here for the card game."

Tarek and I stood outside a nondescript door on the back of a run-down tavern. The evening air was damp and brisk. Both of us were wrapped tightly in woolen cloaks. I could not stop myself from tugging my hood down over my head every few seconds, my focus darting around constantly in a sweep for prying eyes.

Outside the door, a burly man sat on a stool with arms crossed. He was slouched against the wall, a broad-brimmed hat pulled low over his eyes and looking immensely bored.

"Quiet night tonight," the man said.

Tarek's voice dropped to a whisper. "But the tree burns on."

The man tilted his hat up to study the two of us, his eyes sticking on me. "No card game here," he said finally, taking a lazy drag from his pipe.

"Come on, Brother. You know me."

"No card game here."

Tarek glanced over his shoulder, then flipped his cloak away and pulled at the back of his tunic. The fabric bunched upward until the image of spindly roots appeared on his skin, the base of his rebel tattoo.

"That good enough for you?" he hissed as he pulled the fabric back into place. "Let us in."

"I said there's no card game here." The man thrust his chin toward me. "Not for *her*."

I shifted my weight uneasily.

"She's new," Tarek said. "But she brings an offering. A really good one. I'm sure The Father will be pleased."

"I don't care if she brings the keys to the Godsdamned Royal Palace. Until someone that matters tells me she's in, there's no game for her."

"I just need to talk to The Father and show him what she knows. Give us five minutes, Dar—"

"Watch it," the man snapped, rising to his feet. "Remember the rules, or there'll be no game for you either, Brother."

Tarek bristled. "My apologies, Brother. I'm telling you, The Father is going to want to hear what she has to say."

The man looked between the two of us, then came over and stood in front of me. Without warning, he yanked my hood down and grabbed my chin, pulling it closer.

A smarter Solara might have remembered that she was supposed to be acting obediently and loyally to prove herself worthy of these people. A smarter Solara might have let this stranger manhandle her a bit if it convinced him she was not here to cause trouble.

I had always been an act first, think later kind of girl.

I grabbed his wrist and wrenched it from my face, then slammed my other fist into his chest, carefully targeted at the soft flesh below his sternum. Breath wheezed out of him as he doubled over, groaning in pain.

"Solara, stop!" Tarek wrapped an arm around my waist and dragged me away. "What are you doing?" he hissed in my ear.

Though still hunched over, the man's shoulders shook with each rumbling chuckle. "Now there's a woman who knows how to land a punch."

He straightened and took me in again, a threatening gleam in his eyes.

"You," he pointed to Tarek, "go in and speak with The Father." His lips twisted. "She has to stay outside."

Tarek started to protest, but I nudged him forward. "Go on, it's fine."

He hesitated. "Are you sure?"

I made a show of curling my fingers into a fist as I returned the man's smirk. "Don't worry. Me and Tiny here are going to be best friends."

His grin widened.

Tarek gave me a pleading look that was half panic and half admonishment. "Just give me a few minutes." I waved him off and he disappeared inside.

A moment later, the door swung open. A group of three men strode into the alley and formed a semi-circle around me, with Tarek following closely behind. My hands twitched, itching to reach for my weapons.

The man who had positioned himself directly in front of me stepped forward. He was older, near my father's age, his skin rough and marked by scars and the wrinkles of a hard-worn life. Something about him seemed vaguely familiar, though I could not place his face in my memory.

"You're the healer that went into the Royal Palace?" he asked.

"I am."

"A secret passage to enter the property. Did I hear that right?"

My answer came out more certain than I expected. "Yes."

"Can you point it out on a map?"

"I can draw a blueprint of the entire Godsdammed Palace itself." I replied with more confidence than was probably appropriate.

The three men huddled closely, mumbling comments too quiet to hear. I watched the other two react with shock, their lips parting and nostrils flaring, but the man who had initially addressed me showed no reaction.

The weight of self-doubt settled in as I faced them, the false sense of confidence I had carried vanishing in an instant. The years of study and expertise I had earned in my field meant little here. Here, I was nothing and no one. To these three strangers, my only worth lay in the scraps of information I could offer. If that was not enough to impress them, my time as a Protector would be over before it began.

The longer their whispered deliberations stretched on, the stronger my anger grew.

One of them murmured just loudly enough for me to hear. "You can't really be considering letting her in. Don't you realize who she is?"

He continued to watch me, his dark eyes drilling into my own. "I know exactly who she is."

"Then you know why she's off-limits."

He narrowed his gaze. "How old are you, girl?"

"Twenty-two."

"An adult, then. Capable of making your own choices and deciding for yourself where your loyalties lie."

It did not feel like a question, but I nodded nonetheless. "I know what you're fighting for and I know the risks. I'm not afraid to help."

Something tingled against my skin. A chill from the evening air, perhaps, or my conscience warning me of the dangerous line I was about to cross.

I glanced over my shoulder into the darkness of a nearby alley. My eyes squinted as I peered closer, scanning the shadows.

"Yeah," the third man said, drawing my focus back to the group, "I have to agree with my Brother. She's a Hawkthorne. She shouldn't be here. It will cause too many problems when..." He stopped himself, then tipped his head to me with a loaded frown.

The man in the center glanced back at the guard I had socked. "And you, Brother. What do you think? Is she more trouble than she's worth?"

His lips spread into an enormous grin. "Oh, it's up to me, is it?"

I almost groaned.

He sauntered over until he was standing so close that the folds of my cloak brushed against the dark curls spilling free from his half-bared chest. I wanted to choke on the smug arrogance of his face, but I forced myself to keep my chin held high.

His hand rose to my face as if to grab it once again. I pulled back and raised a clenched fist in warning. Even if I had already lost, I would sure as hell go down swinging.

He laughed and dropped his arm. "You've got fight in you, woman. We need more of your kind around here." He turned back to the man in the center. "I say let her in."

"Then it's decided," the man said, a dark smile curving his lips. "Welcome to The Protectors."

19

The Father

From what I had seen of Tarek's rebel friends on our weekend at the tavern, I had expected The Protectors to be an assortment of brusque, overbuilt soldier types. The kind of men who usually swarmed around my father like bees on freshly-bloomed mint.

Although plenty of men of fighting age clumped together, slapping one another's shoulders and laughing raucously as they talked, it was everyone else milling about in the crowded meeting room that caught me by surprise.

Women, lots of them, of various ages, many of whom I recognized. A seamstress who knew my mother well, a few sex workers from Paradise Row, a former classmate chatting with our old teacher. Children too, some not even old enough to have finished school, their faces still round with youth and marked with teenage blemishes. A number of the elderly, too old to fight but perhaps still willing to put their lives on the line in other ways.

There was even one of my own trainees from the healers' center. Lana, who I had spent multiple afternoons with, rushed over to Tarek and began chatting animatedly with him before her eyes landed on me hovering in the background.

Her face drained of color. Mine might well have done the same.

My instinct was to greet her, to step forward and say hello, but something lodged in my chest. What *did* one say in a moment like this? The room was unfamiliar, the rules unspoken, and I was not about to stumble blindly. So I let Tarek take the lead. He slipped into the crowd effortlessly, laughing, leaning into conversations, teasing and smiling as if he had always belonged here. I watched him, envying that ease, and tried to mimic it in the smallest way. Shoulders relaxed, back straight and eyes scanning. We gradually edged toward the back-left corner of the room until we sank into a booth.

A door at the front of the room creaked open and silence fell like a heavy blanket over the assembled crowd. I straightened as one of the men I had seen earlier stepped in, flanked by two other men I had not seen before. Everyone scrambled into the nearest chairs.

"Who are those three men?" I whispered to Tarek, my voice barely audible over the thick silence.

"They're The Father's first , second , and third in command."

"And who's The Father?" I asked, trying to mask my unease with curiosity.

"The one who runs the whole show," Tarek replied with a smirk, as if the answer was the most obvious thing in the world.

Before I could press further the door swung open again and every head in the room swiveled toward the entrance. A figure stepped inside, shrouded in a cloak that seemed to swallow the light. I felt the tension ratchet up a notch, the air thick with anticipation.

The figure stepped to the front and, with one smooth motion, reached up and lowered the hood of the cloak. I felt the world tilt beneath me as Rhea's face emerged from the shadows, her features sharp and composed as ever. Her silver hair was swept back into an intricate braid, adorned with silver threads that matched the brooch at her neck. Beneath the cloak, she wore a fitted tunic of deep charcoal gray, belted at the waist with a wide band of black leather studded with silver rivets. The tunic flared slightly at the hips, the fabric draping elegantly down to her knees, where it met high black boots, laced tightly up the front.

It was not just her attire that struck me. There was an aura about her, something commanding and almost regal. The soft fabric of her cloak, the polished silver accents, and the way she held herself. Everything radiated confidence, dignity and a quiet charisma. She did not need to speak to make her presence felt. It was as if the air shifted when she entered, drawing the attention and respect of everyone around her.

My heart pounded in my chest with a wild rhythm. This was Rhea, *my* Rhea, the woman who had trained me, who had been my mentor and friend. The woman standing before me now was a stranger, someone I had never truly known. The realization hit me like a punch to the gut, knocking the breath from my lungs.

My hands clenched into fists on my lap as I fought to keep my expression neutral. I wanted to react and demand an explanation, but my body would not obey. The world was no longer as I had always known it.

My gaze darted to Tarek, desperate for some kind of confirmation that what I was seeing was real, that I had not completely lost my grip on reality. Tarek just watched her with that same easy confidence and unreadable expression.

Rhea—no, The Father—spoke with a calm authority that cut through the tension like a blade. "Thank you all for coming. We have much to discuss."

I could not tear my eyes away from her, could not stop the tremor that ran through my body as the full weight of my new reality gradually seeped in. Rhea was The Father. The leader of this entire rebellion. Everything I thought I knew about her and the world around me had just shifted. Was it a betrayal? I did not even know. I wanted to scream, run and demand answers, but all I could do was stand there, lost in a suspended reality.

The Father's voice filled the room, strong and unwavering.

"We are getting close to the day. Our efforts have counted and it is all adding up."

She paused, letting her words settle over the gathered crowd. There was no mistaking the steel in her tone and the resolve that underpinned every word she spoke.

"For years, the Aquara have trampled over us, taken our water, killed our children and treated us as less than human. That time is coming to an end."

A murmur of agreement rippled through the room.

"In three days," she continued, "we will plant the seed that will spread its deep roots. A harvest long overdue. It is not an act of destruction, it is justice. The Aquara have lived fat and blind for too long. They will learn what it means to thirst, to feel our pain and to understand what it is that they have taken from us."

My thoughts tangled in a storm of betrayal, surprise and, somewhere deep down, a spark of excitement. This was real. People were willing to risk everything to tip the scales between Aquara and the three other regions of Aetherium. Justice was coming fast. Only moments ago I had been in her house, gawking at her incubator, sipping warm tea. Now here she stood before a large crowd, leading them into war against a formidable adversary.

Just as a moment of panic was about to overwhelm me, Rhea's eyes locked onto mine. Her gaze held mine with a kind of understanding that I had not expected, a gleam in her eyes that spoke of something deeper. It was energizing.

It was as if she could see the turmoil inside me, the doubts and fears that were tearing me apart. She held my gaze, her expression softening ever so slightly. As if to say: *This is who I am. This is who I've always been. Now, what do you stand for?*

The room around us faded into the background, the murmurs and shifting bodies becoming nothing more than white noise. It was just the two of us locked in this silent exchange. I could feel the heat rising in my face, the confusion and the betrayal battling with the part of me that could not reconcile that this was the same woman who had mentored me and guided me through some of the darkest moments of my life.

She broke the gaze first, turning her attention back to the room as if nothing had happened, as if she had not just upended my entire world. "We must remain vigilant," she continued, her voice steady. The calm leader addressed her loyal followers. "The Aquara will not go down without a fight, but neither will we. This is our time. We stand on the brink of something greater than ourselves: real, lasting change. It is because of all of you and your loyalty, dedication and your sacrifices, that we are closer than ever to victory."

The crowd responded with murmurs of agreement, some nodding, others clenching their fists in silent determination. I sat frozen in my seat, my mind racing to catch up with everything that had just unfolded.

Had it all been a lie? Every lesson, every moment we had shared, had it all been just part of a larger plan? Or was there something more, something that I was missing? I searched my memories for clues and signs that could have told me who Rhea truly was. Nothing.

I could hardly breathe as I stood up, my legs unsteady beneath me. The air in the room felt thick and heavy. I needed to get out. Be anywhere but here.

I slipped through the throng of people, my mind a whirlwind of thoughts that I could not make sense of. Each face I passed blurred into the next, their voices merging into an incomprehensible buzz. I kept my head down, moving on autopilot, desperate to escape the suffocating confines of the meeting room.

When I finally pushed through the doors and into the cool night air, I felt a fleeting sense of relief, as if I could finally breathe again. The sky was an inky black, the stars above mere pinpricks of light that seemed so distant and unreachable.

I took two or three deep breaths of the open air when I heard the door creak open behind me. I did not need to look back to know who it was. Her presence was a palpable weight that settled over me.

"Solara dearie—" Rhea's voice was soft and pleading.

I froze for a split second, my heart skipping a beat at the sound of my name on her lips. I was already simmering with emotions of anger, betrayal and confusion. Hearing Rhea's endearing voice made me explode into something fierce and uncontrollable. Without thinking, I bolted.

I heard her call out to me, but I did not stop. I could not stop. I just kept running, my feet aching from pounding against the pavement. The night air whipped against my face and tears blurred my vision. The streets were empty, the world around me eerily quiet. I felt alone.

I did not slow down until I reached home, my chest heaving as I stumbled up the steps to my front door. My hands were trembling so badly that it took me three tries to fit the key into the lock. I slammed the door shut behind me, leaning against it as if I could somehow keep the world outside from crashing in. I stayed there on the cold floor of my entryway, my breath coming in short, uneven gasps as the night stretched on.

20

The King

A WEEK LATER

King Thalor looked much the same as he had on my prior visit, motionless and peaceful beneath the high canopy of his four-poster bed. Out of habit, I took command of the room and strode toward my patient's side, nearly tripping over Darian as he stopped to kneel in respect. I caught myself in time and clumsily mimicked the movement.

"Sorry," I mumbled. What I really wanted to say was, *my unconscious patients aren't usually so fussy about formal greetings.*

Darian gave a single, approving nod, signaling that I could rise. I walked to the King and perched on the bed beside him, watching his chest struggling to rise in uneven bursts. Now that I was closer, it was startling how much his condition had deteriorated. His skin was gray and paper-thin, and his body convulsed with the occasional spasm.

I gingerly laid my palm against his cheek, disheartened to find it clammy despite the thick warmth of the firelit room. A touch to his neck confirmed a pulse that fluttered weakly, as if each beat were being dragged from him against his will.

"It's almost time, isn't it?" Darian asked quietly.

I nodded. "I wish I had better news, but there's not much I can do for him now."

He walked to the other edge of the bed and sat at the King's side, laying a palm on his uncle's chest and staring at him with a troubled look.

"Were you two close?" I asked tentatively.

"That's a difficult question to answer."

His jaw clenched, the familiar stone mask snapping into place. On any other given day, I would have let it go, cursing under my breath at his way of shutting me out.

But today his armor looked fragile—glass instead of steel. If I stared hard enough past the indifference, I could almost see a more vulnerable truth bleeding through the cracks.

"My father and uncle were quite close," he started slowly. "When my uncle became King, my father devoted himself to his reign. I was even bestowed the title of Crown Prince. Then things changed." A crease carved into his brow. "My uncle took me under his wing from a very young age. He became more of a father to me than the man who sired me."

Though his stoic veneer held firm, a heart-wrenching loneliness threaded through his voice. How isolating it must be to be the heir, wondering if any relationship was genuine or simply someone positioning themselves for future gain.

"But?" I prodded.

"Well, we did not always agree..." He paused, staring blankly beyond the walls. I waited for him to continue, but he did not fill the awkward silence even if there was clearly more to tell. His princely composure had snapped back into place.

"That is all I will say on the matter," he finished, tone clipped and proper once more, as if reminding himself who I was and who he was.

Our conversation came to an abrupt halt. A long silence followed, heavier and more awkward than the one before. We both fixed our eyes on the King, doing everything we could to avoid each other's gaze, but I knew Darian's mind was elsewhere, just like mine. Neither of us bothered with empty words just to fill the air.

At last, he spoke. "It's stifling here. Shall we step out onto the balcony?"

I nodded. With a single gesture, he summoned the guards who had been standing out of earshot near the door. They rushed instantly to pull open the towering doors with their panes of blast-proof glass. Without another word, I followed Darian outside.

The balcony stretched wide, overlooking the Palace Gardens three floors below. A palette of crimson, emerald, amber and violet flowers unfurled in rigid geometric patterns across the grounds. It stretched for at least twenty acres, up to the Palace walls that seemed to keep more in than out. It was breathtaking but also suffocating in its perfection. I counted twelve fountains roaring to life with bronze lions and horses frozen mid-leap, endless torrents of water mocking the parched districts beyond the gates. This was only their back garden.

Darian gestured toward the view. "See the paths leading to the central fountain? They divide the grounds into four sections: Aquara, Ignios, Terra and Haren."

"All equal in size and beauty," I said before I could stop myself. I was treading into dangerous territory. Very dangerous territory. Yet Darian only smiled.

I wondered why he had brought me out here, away from the guards. Was it simply to admire the gardens, or had he chosen the moment carefully, to test me or lure me into saying too much? Part of me wanted to ask what he knew of my mother. To press him about the alleyway, about the secrets he seemed to carry so easily while I was left desperate for answers. I nearly asked. I nearly demanded. Instead, I forced the words back down. It was not the right time. Not yet.

"I am grateful to you," he said suddenly, "for saving Vira's life."

"It is my duty," I replied. "I am a healer."

"How did you do it? Vira mentioned… a glowing light. Magic."

I stiffened. "Is that why you brought me out here?" I said calmly. "To accuse me of sorcery?"

His gaze did not waver. "No. I wished for a conversation free from the presence of the guards. A conversation without limitation."

"No limitations?" I echoed, sharper than intended. The fountains gnawed at me, water spilling endlessly while my people in Sand City suffered. My temper made me reckless. I momentarily forgot I stood before the heir to the throne.

"Yes," he said evenly. "You may ask me anything, as I may you." The offer unsettled me. Honesty was perilous in a place like this, yet he dangled it before me like bait. Before I could stop myself, the words slipped free.

"If King Thalor passes, does the Crown pass to you?"

Without the guards, Darian spoke differently. "It is impossible to know."

"But everyone assumes it is you, do they not? Succession favors the strongest and you are the strongest."

"Our power isn't so easily measured."

I forced a brittle smile. "I am Haren, Prince Darian. Spare me the false modesty."

A wry smile tugged at his lips, edged with sadness. "Yes. It's expected to pass to me."

It was not difficult to picture him on the throne. He already carried himself with a quiet authority that bent the air around him. And yet, unlike most Aquara, there was something gentler there too. He treated the Palace Healers with more dignity than any other Aquara I had met.

"And what kind of King do you intend to be?" I asked.

His head tilted, and he answered with an unrelated question. "Do you think my uncle is a bad King?"

I bit the inside of my cheek. Best not to unleash fury upon the man he had just called a father figure.

"I am a powerless mortal, remember. What insight can I possess into Kings?"

"Tell me." His voice was quiet but pressing. "Be candid."

A groan slipped from me. Speaking the truth here could cost my life. Yet his eyes remained curious, perhaps, or calculating. Would I ever again have the ear of the future King of Aquara?

"He has enacted cruel laws," I said finally. "Laws that harm children."

"The prohibition on intermarriage," he stated, not as a question.

I inclined my head.

"You believe that this law ought to be abolished?" he asked.

"No child should perish because of their parents or their heritage," I said, my voice firm.

Darian's expression did not change. His gaze lingered a heartbeat too long, his silence pressing heavier than any words. When he finally spoke, his voice was impossible to read.

"Even if that's the cost required to keep your realm powerful?"

"If the death of innocents is a cost you're willing to pay, then you don't deserve to be powerful."

Pale blue light flared brightly behind his eyes, but Darian did not answer. In the ensuing quiet, we both turned our attention back to the garden.

"You haven't been around the Palace much recently," Darian said finally, his voice clipped. "We could use additional healers."

"I took some time away."

"Any particular reason?"

I let out a short, humorless laugh. "Do I need to remind you what happened last time?" My mind went back to the chaos that followed after I vanished with Princess Vira for the entire afternoon.

He gave a curt nod. "Right. That didn't go over well. You have a habit of bending the rules." A faint smile crossed his face. "But you're good at your job."

"I know," I said, meeting his gaze. "That's why I came back."

"You are," he acknowledged. "I saw how you managed my sister when she was frightened," he added, gesturing toward his uncle inside, "and how you're attending to him now, despite your dislike for him."

I turned my face away.

He craned his neck, trying to catch my eye. "I think you have a rare gift for seeing a person as *who* they are, not just *what* they are."

My voice went quiet. "If you knew me better, you might think differently."

It was the most I dared to reveal.

A loud knock rang out at the chamber door.

"Enter," Darian barked, his eyes still locked on mine.

Two guards opened the balcony doors again and saluted Darian. Upon Darian's gesture, one of the guards came forward and leaned in to whisper something in his ear. He swore under his breath, then turned fully to the guard, exchanging a few inaudible words.

Without another glance at me, Darian stalked toward the door with the second guard trailing behind. "I need to handle a situation. Stay here. Don't run this time, Miss Hawkthorne. Do you understand?"

"You're leaving me here? Alone? With the King?" I called after him, disbelief sharpening my voice.

Darian did not even slow down. "No. He will be here." He gestured toward the far corner of the room.

I turned, startled, to find a figure I had not noticed until now, silent, imposing, and clad in armor that seemed to blend into the shadows. He stood perfectly still, like a sentinel carved from stone.

"That," Darian said sharply, "is the King's Royal Guard. His sole purpose is to protect the King, even at the cost of his life. He'll ensure you don't do anything… regrettable."

Without a backward glance, Darian strode out of the room. "I'll be back soon."

The heavy door slammed shut behind him, leaving the guard, me and my knives alone with the King of Aquara.

21

The Final Breath

I stared at the closed door for a full minute.

I considered waiting for Darian in the main salon, convincing the guards to escort me to the front parlor, or even offering up my weapons until he returned.

The truth was, I no longer knew how I felt about anything.

A month ago, I had been focused. I had clear, attainable goals:

Find my mother. Protect Kian. Serve as the Palace Healer. Help The Protectors.

I may not have loved my place in the world, but at least I knew where it was.

Now, my future felt empty.

I stared at King Thalor, sprawled before me. Even on his deathbed, a faint aura of power clung to him. Weakened, yes, but still commanding and still imposing. What must it feel like to be the most powerful person in the realm? Today, he was no fearsome child of the Gods. Today, he was just an old man, slipping away. Alone.

Suddenly, a spasm rippled through his body and then another. His eyelids flickered delicately, as if lost in a dream. His breathing was rapid, far too fast and far too shallow. It would not be much longer now.

I took his hand, laying my palm against his wrist until our pulses aligned. It was an old healer's trick: when all medicine failed, sometimes a cherished touch could persuade a fading heart to match the stronger beat of its beloved. I might not be King Thalor's nearest and dearest, but at the moment, he and I were all each other had.

I gave his wrist a gentle squeeze and softly whispered the sacred prayer of Eternal Rest:

"O gentle soul, now take your flight,

Into the arms of endless light.

Your journey done, your burdens cease,

May you find eternal peace.

No fear shall mar your tranquil way,

As night surrenders to the day.

With grace, ascend to realms above,

Enfolded in eternal love.

In sacred peace, your spirit soars,

Where pain and sorrow are no more.

Rest now in the divine embrace,

In heaven's light, find your place."

As the final word fell from my lips, a crackle of energy passed between us, a static shock that made every hair on my arms stand on end. The King's gnarled fingers seized mine. No longer feeble and frail, his grip was an iron shackle chaining me at his side.

His eyes flew open, fixing on me like he had been watching me even in sleep. Dark, deep-sea blue. Startlingly clear. Lucid.

Something more than lucid. Seeing more than me. Seeing *into* me.

"You," he croaked, his voice hoarse from months of atrophy. "I did not believe them when they said you existed. You've finally found me."

I wrenched backward, yanking my arm, trying and failing to break free from his hold. "No—I'm sorry. I—please, let me go."

"They told me you would come for me."

"What? Who?"

The iron-clad guard, who had stood still as stone until now, shifted. His gaze sharpened as he moved toward the bed.

"They said your blood would burn the Palace and lay waste to our borders."

I leaned in, gently shushing him, trying to soothe his sudden outburst. The poor man was lost to hallucinations. "Everything's alright," I murmured. "I'm not going to hurt you."

His skin began to glow with an unnatural light. The King gasped, his grip on me tightening. "I am not afraid, Devourer of Crowns. Ravager of Vengeance. My dear daughter."

Oh, he was definitely delusional.

I stroked his arm gently, cooing in a soothing voice. "Your nephew, Prince Darian, I'll go get him. Just let go of my hand, alright?"

"Darian," he breathed. Brighter and brighter he blazed, like the final flare of a dying star. His eyes bulged wide, the vivid blue of his irises fading to a dusky smoke.

His throat made a strangled noise and then his voice changed. It sounded older, impossibly older.

Unearthly.

The guard reacted instantly, unsheathing his sword in a single, fluid motion. The steel glinted dangerously in the dim light as he stepped forward, his voice sharp and commanding. "Step back! What have you done?"

Weak protests tumbled from my lips, fractured and useless. "I—I did not—" I stammered, my feet frozen, my mind a whirlwind of terror and disbelief.

The King's lips moved again, but the words were no longer his own. "Give him our gift, Daughter of the Forgotten. When the end has come and the blood has spilled, give our gift to my faithful heir and tell him this is my command."

The King's back arched, his chest lifting at an unnatural angle before collapsing back onto the bed. His hand went limp, finally releasing me from his grasp.

My heart thundered with unease. I staggered backward, tripping over a nearby chair. I crashed to the ground and my father's blade tumbled from its sheath, clattering across the stone floor. I snatched it up, holding it defensively.

The King took a shuddering breath, a rattling exhale, the kind I had only ever heard when death was imminent.

The glow faded from his skin along with what little color remained. His pallor turned ashen, his expression contorted in agony and his mouth fixed wide in a silent scream.

"Blessed Gods, what did you do?" The guard's voice was a low growl. He stood rigid, his sword gleaming and menacing in the dim light. His horrified gaze jumped between me and the King.

Oh, this wasbad. "Nothing," I said quickly, scrambling to my feet. "It—it happens sometimes. When death is near, they can—"

"What's going on here?" Darian's voice.

So bad. So, so bad.

Darian appeared in the main salon with two more guards, all three of them staring at my hands.

My quivering hands, clutching a steel dagger in a white-knuckled grip. I did not even realize until that instant that I was holding my dagger, having instinctively reached for it when the guard reached for his sword. My father's words came to mind: *Train until it becomes instinct and you won't have to think the day the fight comes to you.*

To someone who had just walked in, it surely looked like I had been about to do something evil. Something treasonous.

"The King has passed, Prince Darian," I said, forcing my voice to stay steady. "A natural death. I did all I could."

Darian pushed past the guards and moved to King Thalor's side. He took one look at the King's contorted expression, then yanked back the blankets and searched his body for wounds.

"I did not hurt him," I blurted out.

The guard's voice cut through the room like a blade. "That girl is evil," he snarled, pointing a trembling finger at me. "She did some sort of sorcery on the King."

"Sorcery?" I shook my head so hard it felt like it might snap. "I swear, I didn't do anything!"

I looked at Darian, desperate for some sign of belief, but the dark suspicion I had seen in him before had returned. The worst part was that it hurt. He had no reason to believe me, plenty of reasons not to. Watching Darian glare at me like I had killed a man I barely knew twisted something small and bitter in my chest. For a moment, I had foolishly thought we might have been friends.

Darian silently finished inspecting the King's body. I turned away and stared at the wall, trying to hold back the emotions squeezing at my chest. Once satisfied the King was unharmed, Darian paused. His features tightened as he turned and started toward me.

I spoke slowly. "I'm so sorry."

Darian looked away, his eyes sharp and unyielding.

A long beat of silence passed.

"You're free to go, Solara," he said quietly.

I packed my supplies, my hands trembling slightly, and left the room. I had to fight the urge to run, settling instead for a hurried jog down the winding staircase, two steps at a time. I had seen too much today. Heard too much.

The last light of the day's Sun was clinging to the silhouette of the Palace towers before slipping away. It was as if the sky knew the King's time had ended.

Devourer of Crowns. Ravager of Vengeance. My dear daughter.

What in the four realms could that have meant?

I had done everything by the book, exactly as my mother would have. I cleansed the wounds, stabilized the King's pulse and whispered the prayers she had drilled into me for years. Every precaution. Every herb. Every measured touch.

As I neared the main entry, the guards at the door noticed the dagger still clutched in my hand. Their sneers sharpened.

"Watch it, witch," one spat, stepping forward with teeth bared.

"You think that knife makes you brave?" another hissed, circling me like a predator sizing up prey.

Ungrateful fools. I had bent over backward to save their precious King when they could have sent any healer. Any other healer. Now, they looked at me like I had murdered him for sport.

I was nearly to the Palace Gates when Darian's voice rang out behind me.

"Solara, wait."

I turned, forcing myself to take a slow breath and smooth my expression. His grief hung around him like a storm cloud and I had no right to meet it with my own anger.

"I'm truly sorry, Darian. I did all I could," I said quietly.

He looked at me, hesitant and shook his head. "No, it's not that—"

BOOM.

A deafening crack split the air.

22

The Bombing

The walls of the Palace rattled.

"What in the Sun Goddess's name was that?" Darian muttered.

BOOM. BOOM.

The two of us jolted and crouched low.

"Thunder?" I guessed. "I did not see storm clouds earlier, but maybe..."

Darian shook his head, a deep crease forming between his brows. "I've heard that sound before. That was an explosion."

My stomach dropped. "As in... a bomb?"

He rose quickly, scanning the grounds. After a moment, he nodded and extended a finger. "There."

I scrambled to his side, craning my neck to see.

BOOM.

Close to us, no more than a few hundred meters away, a billowing swirl of flame leapt into the air. Puffy clouds of smoke glowed with the light of the fires below, an orange smear against the ink-dark sky.

"The Palace is being attacked," Prince Darian said slowly.

The air felt impossible to breathe, too weighty to pull into my lungs.

Air pressed against my chest like lead. Every breath felt borrowed. My mind scrambled, piecing together the impossible. Three days.

Three days ago, The Protectors had said they would strike in three days and I, careless me, I had walked Tarek through the Palace as if it were a museum, laughing at the sheer audacity of it all. He had listened to every detail, leaning in, and I had never imagined it would matter.

BOOM.

I did this. This is my fault.

"I—I have to go," I stammered, stumbling backward.

Prince Darian turned sharply. "What? Go where? You're not going towards that fire!"

I recoiled violently from his hand.

I did this.

"I have to go." My voice was shaky and hoarse.

"Solara, no."

I ran.

The vermilion flames already engulfed the east side of the Palace. My stomach dropped. That was the side I had asked Vira about, the side of the Royal Armory my father, a former Ignios soldier, had always praised, even though he had never actually been inside. He had a particular fascination with the Armory's Pyrefang Cannons: their deadly reach, their precision and the stories he loved to tell. I had only asked Princess Vira about it out of curiosity, innocently picking at the edges of his obsession.

How had they gotten in? I could hear each thump of my own heart pounding. The secret entrance. My stupid, careless words.

The loss of life would be catastrophic. So many of them would be people I had met.

Eloisa. Princess Vira. Oh Gods, Princess Vira.

Bile rose in my throat. I clamped my hand over my mouth and forced a long inhale of air through my nose.

With my healer's satchel still slung tightly across my shoulder, my boots continued to hit the soil.

I ran.

My thighs burned with effort, my lungs tightened with a need for air, but I dared not slow, not even for a second. Two thoughts blared through my mind like a relentless metronome, keeping pace with my pounding steps.

I did this. This is my fault.

Princess Vira and Eloisa are going to die because of me.

This is my fault.

"Solara?"

It took me a moment to register.

The voice was very familiar.

I could not stop, could not slow down, not even for—

"Solara? Stop running, it's me!"

One of the men jogged forward, stepping into my path. I was on the outskirts of the Palace Gardens, running along the tall spiring gates. With the last light fading from the sky, I could not make out the details of his face.

"Can't stop," I forced out through wheezing breaths. "Please—move!"

"Solara—it's me, Tarek."

My steps faltered, then slowed, but I did not stop. I could not. I had to keep going, to get to the fire, to help them.

Tarek reached out and seized my arms, hauling me to a stop against my will.

"What. The hell. Are you doing. Out here?" I screamed in his face. Yet, I knew exactly what he was doing.

"I could ask you the same thing," Tarek replied, his tone strained.

I pointed a trembling hand toward the distant inferno. "Explosion. Fire. Going to help." My chest shuddered as I gasped for air.

He gave me a strange look, then glanced over his shoulder at The Protectors assembled behind him, their faces still shrouded by the darkness.

Tarek's hands clamped too hard on my shoulders. His voice dropped low. "Solara, go home. Don't worry about the fire."

I shoved him back, anger flaring. "You *betrayed me*! I was telling you as a friend! I trusted you! I thought you'd ask me before sharing all these details!" My voice cracked, shaking with disbelief. "The secret entrance… the Pyrefang Cannons… everything I told you in confidence. Why like this, Tarek?"

He flinched, but did not answer.

"You don't understand!" I shouted, shaking him. "There could be people dying right now! I need to—"

"Solara." There was a deadly gravity to his features. "Listen to me. Go home and stay there. Forget you saw the fire. What's about to happen tonight will be a lot worse."

I opened my mouth to protest, but a muted boom interrupted me. The ground rumbled beneath our feet. The fiery cloud ballooned higher, brighter and angrier.

Quiet snickers rippled through the group. One of the shadowed men clapped another on the back. Even the corner of Tarek's lips twitched upward.

My body went still.

The world went still.

That was when I noticed them. A group of imposing, burly men advancing from the shadows, each gripping a weapon with lethal intent. Gleaming swords, menacing axes, spiked maces and serrated daggers. The firelight flickered across their bodies, revealing The Protectors' tattoo seared into their flesh. Some had it inked across their forearms, others on their necks, chests, even the sides of their shaved heads.

One of the men, larger and more menacing than the rest, stepped forward with predatory grace. As the blaze flared, its orange glow lit his scarred face and cold, unyielding eyes.

"Sister Solara," the man said, his smile lazy and triumphant. "The fight tonight is as much yours as ours. We couldn't have done this without you."

My eyes swept over the group, landing on two men I recognized from the tavern meeting days ago. Then they flicked to the pair of carts, both piled high and covered with tarps.

They were not just going to bomb the Palace. They were preparing for war.

Tarek glanced toward the tall man. He paused, then subtly shook his head.

"Brother Tarek is right," the large man said firmly. "You should return home and speak of this to no one."

A horrible sense of dread settled in my chest, cold and absolute.

"I can't. People might be wounded! Children. I need to go." I stepped back, trying to pull away, but Tarek's hands clamped down, holding me firm.

The tall man's smile faded. He stepped forward, his tone colder now. "We can't let you do that, Sister. It's best if no Harens are seen near the target."

I tried to free myself again, but Tarek's grip only tightened. His fingers dug painfully into my shoulders. I stared at him in shock.

"Solara," he began, his voice low.

"Get your hands off me, Tarek."

He did not budge.

Around us, the others silently closed in, forming a circle around us.

Tarek's face shifted, pleading and conflicted. "Don't make me do this, Solara. We've been planning this for weeks. We can't risk you blowing the whole operation."

"Don't make you do what?" I hissed.

The circle of Protectors edged inward, closing around me like a tightening noose. Their eyes, sharp and mistrustful, watched my every move.

My heart thundered.

Six of them. All larger and stronger than me.

There was no way I could take them, not all of them. If they wanted, they could grab me and drag me back to Sand City kicking and screaming. My father's words broke through my roaring thoughts.

What have I taught you about fighting an opponent much stronger than you?

He had prepared me for this.

Despite the panic rising in my chest, I worked my face into a mask of calm. Just then, a sharp clattering of armor echoed across the stone courtyard. Prince Darian burst from the shadows, his face etched with urgency. Behind him marched a battalion of Royal Guards, their armor gleaming cold in the torchlight.

"Solara, get back here right now!" Prince Darian's voice cut through the night like a blade. "These men are dangerous."

One of The Protectors behind Tarek—the tallest, the one who carried himself like a commander—stepped forward. His lips curled into a cruel sneer as the guards advanced. "Well, look who decided to join the party," he spat, his voice thick with disdain. His eyes flicked to me, and the sneer deepened. "I have to thank you again, Solara. If it weren't for you, we would never have made it this far."

I felt a chill run down my spine as his words hung in the air like a curse. He stepped closer, gaze fixed on me. "You led us right to the Prince. I couldn't have planned it better myself."

Prince Darian reached me, his hand closing around my arm. He pulled me back as the tension in the air became almost suffocating. "Solara," he said, low and serious. "We need to leave, now."

The Protector was not finished. He turned toward his men and gestured broadly as if hosting some grotesque performance. "Look at her, boys. The perfect example of a traitor."

The Protectors shifted, their grips tightening on their weapons. In their eyes, I saw everything. Loyalty, fear, doubt and resolve.

I turned to Tarek, barely recognizing the man in front of me. I pushed him hard in the chest, my voice shaking with anger and disbelief. "Innocent children, Tarek? What have you become? This is madness!"

Tarek's eyes, once warm, were now hollow and cold, like something inside him had died. "If this is the cost of freedom," he said quietly, "I'm willing to pay it."

"Tarek, don't do this," I pleaded. "Justice doesn't have to be achieved this way."

The tall Protector chuckled darkly, a sound that sent a shiver through me. "Oh, but it does. You see, Solara, the world doesn't change without a little bloodshed. Tonight, we'll see *just* how much blood it takes."

The firelight cast an eerie glow on his face as he raised his sword high, the blade gleaming ominously. "This is what freedom demands and you," he added, eyes narrowing as they locked onto Prince Darian, "you're about to pay the price."

Then, with a guttural roar that seemed to shake the very earth, The Protector bellowed, "FIGHT!"

Chaos erupted at the foot of the Royal Palace. The Protectors charged forward, weapons drawn, driven by a fierce desperation that made them almost feral. The clamor of steel meeting steel filled the air as The Protectors clashed violently with the Royal Guards. The night was alive with the sounds of battle: the grunts of men locked in combat, the clash of swords and cries of the wounded.

The Royal Guards' ranks swelled with reinforcements and surged forward, pushing The Protectors back against the imposing iron gates. Prince Darian grabbed my arm, pulling me away with a desperate urgency. "Solara, we need to go. Now!"

As I stumbled back, Tarek's gaze locked onto Darian's hand gripping my arm, a flicker of anger igniting in his eyes. "You've become one of them," he spat, his voice thick with betrayal. "I don't even recognize you anymore."

I stood paralyzed, torn between the man who had been my closest friend and the one who held the secrets I desperately needed. My voice trembled as I tried to speak, but all I managed was a broken plea. "Please..."

Darian had dragged me far enough from the gates that I knew Tarek could not hear me anymore, but it did not matter. I was not even sure what I was pleading for, mercy, understanding or perhaps just an end to the nightmare unraveling before my eyes.

The battle raged on around us, the air thick with the smell of blood and sweat. Tarek, consumed by a fury I had never seen before, pushed through the gates and tore himself away from the desperate cries of The Protectors. He raised his sword and charged back into the fray, each strike more savage than the last.

"Tarek, no! Stay back!" I screamed, my voice barely audible over the chaos. I fought against Prince Darian's grip, my heart pounding in my chest. I saw it all in agonizing slow motion, the glint of a spearhead and the swift, deadly thrust from a Royal Guard standing just inside the gates.

The spear drove straight through the iron bars and into Tarek's chest.

"NOOO!"

Tarek's scream of agony cut through the night, piercing the air like a death knell. He staggered, his hand outstretched toward me, fingers trembling as he tried to grasp the iron bars of the gate for support. Blood seeped from the wound, dark and viscous, staining the cold stone beneath him.

He fell to his knees, his hand still reaching out for me from behind the gate, his face twisted in pain and shock. His body crumpled to the ground, his fingers slipping from the bars as his strength failed him. The gate, now a barrier that could never be crossed again, separated us forever.

The world around me blurred, the sounds of battle fading into a distant roar as black spots clouded my vision. Tarek, the boy I had grown up with in Sand City, was *gone*.

It came crashing down on me, suffocating my lungs and body. I could not breathe.

23

The Fire

I had spent hours at the Royal Infirmary with my chest heaving and lungs tight, where Prince Darian had dropped me before returning with the Royal Guard to douse the fire and keep The Protectors from storming the Palace. Shock had hollowed me out and left me numb. The Protectors. The bombings. Tarek. Tarek, dear Gods. The memory clawed at me. The red spattering across the marble, his body crumpling with a dull thud. It had all happened so fast I questioned whether it had really happened at all, or if I was still trapped in a nightmare I could not wake from.

Relief hit me when I learned Princess Vira and Eloisa had survived, but everything else was a blur. I did not know if the fire still burned; I only knew the infirmary floor was alive with suffering. Nurses carried groaning bodies on stretchers, their shoes clattering against the marble, voices sharp with urgency. Some bodies were still warm, some already cold. Death had visited the Royal Palace, and its shadow hung over everything, impossible to shake.

My stomach twisted when a nurse burst through the doors, breathless, eyes wide. "The fire has engulfed the entire Armory! We need more hands!"

I froze for a fraction of a second, letting the words sink in. The entire Armory? My chest tightened. My father had once bragged about every inch of that place. Every cannon, every blade. Now it was on fire. The Protectors had taken what they wanted. I could only imagine the royal weapons, melted, twisted and destroyed.

There was nothing I could do about it. I was a Palace Healer, that was my purpose. If I could stop even a single life from slipping away, I would. Even more guilt would come later but, for now, I still had a chance to stop the hemorrhaging. Literally and figuratively. I had to make sure no one was left in the fire.

"Take me there," I told her.

The Royal Guard had formed an expansive perimeter around the site of the attack, their spears and shields glinting in the flickering light. Smoke coiled into the sky like dark fingers, carrying the acrid stench of burning wood and metal. The nurse, whose name I learned was Selene, led me through a narrow path between scorched statues and crumbling walls.

We reached the Armory. Flames devoured its entrance, licking the stone and wood with a feral hunger. I drew in a ragged breath. "Selene, you should go," I said, my voice rough and shaking. "Go help the others. I… I can manage."

After a tense moment, she nodded, reluctantly tearing herself away. "Be careful," she whispered.

It was not the searing heat inside the Armory that I could not stand but the smoke curling and crowding against my lungs, slowly suffocating me until red-hot pain scattered my thoughts.

A cookpot of sizzling oil.

Red-hot iron liquefied over a blacksmith's forge.

The flaming surface of the Godsdamned Sun.

The Armory's walls and floor were made of stone, likely the only reason any part of the building still stood, but the tall wooden rafters had become one incandescent cloud of fire. The heat radiated downward with a palpable weight, turning the air into a suffocating soup that resisted every movement, like wading through liquid fire.

The ground ahead was mostly clear, though littered with flaming debris. Overhead, the remaining beams crackled like a winter hearth, once a sound of comfort, now a fiery death that could collapse on me at any moment.

I crawled along the floor as quickly as I could, the collar of my tunic pulled over my mouth to filter the blackened air.

"Hello?" I screamed, my voice already ragged from inhaling the acrid smoke. "Can anyone hear me? Please, call out!"

Silence.

I crawled down the path the woman had described, my fingers brushing against the rough walls of the main corridor. At the entrance to a vast storeroom, a golden plaque engraved with the word '*Blades*' lay discarded on the floor. The roof had partially collapsed, allowing the cool night air to cut through the haze and thin the choking smog. The shelves along the walls were eerily empty and several wooden crates lay overturned, their contents scattered or missing. A few knives littered the ground, the pale gemstones in their dark wooden handles flickering in the unsteady firelight.

Then, I spotted a pair of boots jutting out from behind a crate. My heart seized as I scrambled toward the figure slumped on its side, my pulse thundering in my ears and my prayers a frantic chant.

I grasped his shoulder and heaved him onto his back, only to recoil with a gasp of horror. The man's eyes, wide and lifeless, stared at nothing, his mouth frozen in a silent plea. Blood had soaked through his tunic, pooling around the deep, vicious gash that had nearly severed his throat.

Not burned. Not suffocated by smoke.

Murdered.

My thoughts snapped back to The Protectors I had encountered at the Palace Gates and the two heavily loaded carts they had been hauling. I glanced again at the empty shelves and overturned crates, a grim realization settling over me.

What had I expected? That The Protectors would politely knock and ask for what they wanted?

I continued to crawl through the room, searching for survivors but finding only two more dead guards. One lay headless, his body crumpled in a pool of blood, while the other had been torn apart by an explosion, his remains barely recognizable.

At least four Palace Guards' lives were extinguished in brutal ways. Four people who never stood a chance.

Killing had seemed so easy when I faced the Aquara man in the alley. After watching him murder that defenseless mortal woman, I was ready to end his life in an instant. My rage was so intense and so consuming that snuffing out his existence hardly felt like a choice.

It was the same blinding fury Tarek had felt after witnessing the Aquara man on horseback trample the Haren boy, a burning need for vengeance and justice that scorched away everything else.

That day in the alley, I had believed I was ready—like Tarek— to become a Protector, to join the war and to do whatever was necessary to protect my people. To kill, if it came to that.

These guards had done nothing wrong except being Aquara in the wrong place at the wrong time.

War means death, pain, misery and sacrifice. It means making choices that will haunt you for the rest of your life, my father had said.

If this was the kind of killing that war required, I was not ready and I never would be.

I collapsed onto the floor beside the fallen guards as smoke and heat closed in around me. For a moment, it felt as if the burning roof had truly caved in, the full weight of everything I had endured the past months crashing down all at once.

The air was thin and my mind was just as hazy. Every new thought seemed to claw its way up from a pit of bubbling tar. I tried to push myself to my feet, but each time I summoned the last of my strength, my eyes would lock onto the lifeless eyes of the body beside me, and the weight of all the blood on my hands would drag me back down.

Maybe it was best to just stay here, curl up and wait for the inevitable. It would be a painful way to die but maybe that was exactly what I deserved.

I did this. This is my fault.

The fight drained out of me. I sank to the floor, a tear burning its way down my cheek as I closed my eyes and let the darkness take me.

Fight.

My eyes snapped open.

How long had I been lying here? Was I dead?

My exposed skin throbbed, swollen, tender and almost sizzling against the blistering stone floor.

Fight.

"No," I whispered, my voice weak and cracked.

I had made my choice. This was the end. There was no point in resisting, no point in—

Fight.

A sudden surge of energy tore through my veins, an icy blast that cooled my burning skin and made me recoil from the scorching tiles beneath me.

"By the Gods," I cursed, forcing myself upright. "I can't even die in peace."

The voice prowled inside me like a restless predator, snapping its jaws and driving me to move, to escape and to fight for my life. All the things my mind and heart had already given up on.

I inhaled deeply, surprised to find my lungs clear and unharmed. The room was still thick with swirling, noxious smoke. I should have lost consciousness by now.

Fight. Fight. Fight.

"Fine," I growled, dragging myself to my feet. "I'm up. Leave me alone."

As I stood upright, the air felt molten, hotter than it had been on the ground. Yet somehow, the searing heat no longer bothered me. A cold tingling spread from my chest, running up into my head and down my arms and legs, numbing me against the inferno around me.

"I've gone insane," I thought. "Two months off the Emberberry, and I've really lost it."

I stumbled out of the room and wavered in the corridor, my smoke-fogged mind struggling to orient itself in the smoldering darkness.

As if the Gods themselves were listening, a flaming chunk of collapsing rafters crashed to my right, narrowly missing my head. Another, larger piece followed, slamming into the ground beside it. I lurched to the left, cursing under my breath.

A quick glance upward told me I did not have much time before the rest of the roof gave way. If I was going to act, it had to be now.

I broke into a jog down the hall. "Hello?" I called, my voice hoarse and raw. "Is anyone still alive?"

Over the roar of the crackling flames and crashing debris, I barely caught a weak cry almost lost in the chaos.

"Hello?" I shouted again, louder this time, desperation creeping into my voice. "Can you hear me?"

"Please... Help."

My heart raced.

"Keep talking! I'm coming."

"H-help me... Blessed Gods, please... I don't want to die..."

I found them in a side room off the main corridor, one man collapsed on the ground, the other pinned beneath a massive beam. His hips were crushed under the weight, his legs twisted at unnatural angles that made my stomach turn.

His eyes met mine and they were filled with despair. He did not need to hear how hopeless it was. "Please don't leave me," he pleaded. "Please... save me."

"I will. You're going to be okay," I assured him. There was no way I could lift the beam alone. Maybe if I went back, got one of the Aquara guards and convinced the others to hold the entrance open long enough for us to—

A barrage of rubble crashed down the hallway, followed by a wave of flame surging through the corridor and spilling into the room. Instinctively, I threw myself over the injured man, shielding him from the fiery blast.

Fight.

The voice pulsed through my mind, sending a cold shiver across my skin. A hiss echoed in the room and I glanced up to see steam rising toward the ceiling.

Definitely going insane.

"What's your name?" I asked.

"Perthe."

"Alright, Perthe. Can you push this beam off your leg?"

He shook his head. "Can't. Too weak."

I turned to the man sprawled beside him. A quick check of his pulse confirmed he was alive, but no amount of shaking or slapping could bring him back to consciousness.

This was bad. Even if I managed to free Perthe, I would have to carry both of them through a deadly gauntlet of fire and falling debris. I was not strong enough. The weight of hopelessness threatened to crush me. I could not do this. They were both going to die and it was all my f—

Fight, the voice snapped, cutting through my spiraling thoughts.

Right. No time for doubt.

I gripped the wooden beam pinning Perthe, wincing as the still-glowing embers scorched my skin. Taking a deep breath, I threw my weight against it, desperate to shift it even an inch.

In my days as a healer, I had heard stories of Harens who tapped into some hidden well of inhuman strength in moments of crisis. Frantic mothers who single-handedly lifted overturned carriages off their children, or delicate ladies hauling a fallen horse away from their beloved trapped beneath. There was something about the terror of losing someone we love that coated your bones in steel and filled your veins with fire, giving us the will to face death with defiance and push our bodies beyond anything we thought possible.

Perthe was the furthest thing from someone I loved, but it was the only explanation for how the massive beam, far too large for me to move, began to budge. Inch by inch it shifted until it finally slid free from his mangled legs. The charred wood thudded to the ground, sending a cloud of glowing embers swirling around us.

Perthe cried out at the movement. Whether from pain or relief I could not tell.

"Can you put any weight on your legs?" I asked.

He tried to lift himself, but his chest barely left the ground before he collapsed. His face twisted in agony. "I'm sorry," he whispered, his eyes clouding with the familiar defeat.

"It's alright. You're going to be fine." I glanced between him and the unconscious man, a plan beginning to form. "We're getting out of here. All three of us."

A spark of hope flickered in his expression. "We are?"

"We are. But—" I grimaced. "—this is going to hurt like hell."

Perthe nodded determinedly and forced himself upward again. A tortured cry tore from his throat, but he managed to prop himself up on his elbows. "I can take it," he panted.

"Good." I grasped the arms of the unconscious man, dragging him closer to Perthe until their bodies were neatly aligned. "I can't carry you both, but I might be able to drag you. We're going to use your friend here as a makeshift stretcher. Can you lie on top of him?"

Perthe nodded once more, his face set with grim determination. He gritted his teeth, choking back his screams as I wrapped my arms around his chest and heaved his body across the other man's back. I winced, carefully arranging his broken legs and shattered hips until the two were stacked together.

"Hold on as tight as you can," I said as I wrapped my arms around the unconscious man's waist, securing him tightly.

I planted my heels against the stone floor, bracing myself, and threw my weight forward with a strained grunt.

My heart pounded with cautious hope as I felt the men behind me inch forward, only to sink in despair as we ground to a halt.

I took a deep breath and pushed again. A few more feet, then another stop. A scream tore from my throat as I plunged deep within myself, scraping the edges of my soul for any last shred of strength.

Another foot. Then another. Then another.

We moved like this for what felt like an eternity. Every inch was a grueling battle. Even Perthe, with his brutally shattered body, did what he could, pushing against the stone floor with his palms.

After every push, I was left deflated and utterly drained, certain I had nothing left to give. Each time, just as I was ready to collapse, The Voice inside me surged to life, unlocking some hidden reserve of defiance. Flames licked the walls as we passed, falling debris searing my arms with blisters and burns—though I barely noticed. All I felt was the relentless pounding of my heart and the insistent call of The Voice driving me forward.

When a cool breeze finally brushed my cheek, it felt like a splash of spring water in the Ignios deserts. Through the smoke and flames, I glimpsed an opening to the starry night beyond and, in that opening, a face—bright blue-gray eyes.

"Solara!"

Darian.

His voice was hoarse, a stark contrast to the icy calm I had always known.

Like a candle snuffed out, the last of my energy vanished. I collapsed to my knees with a painful, heavy thud.

"Darian," I croaked. "I can't…"

"Stay there. Stay strong. I'm coming."

Shouts echoed through the chaos. Feet shuffled. Metal and wood groaned as they shifted.

"I'm coming for you," he shouted again.

He reached me, his hands firm yet gentle as he guided me toward the exit. Then, without wasting another second, Prince Darian knelt beside the two men, his fingers slipping under their limp arms. Together, we gripped their battered bodies, the weight of them almost too much to bear. With every ounce of strength left in us, we pulled, inch by agonizing inch, the heat of the flames licking at our backs as the exit loomed closer.

"Pull—now!" I yelled. "Pull!"

I felt the sting of fresh air before I saw it, cool and sharp as it filled my lungs. Then, the dim light of the outside world broke through the smoke, and I knew we had finally made it outside.

A breathless laugh bubbled up from my chest. I had done it. They were safe. Severely wounded, probably forever scarred, but alive.

I forced myself to my feet, swaying unsteadily on bone-weary legs, and staggered forward.

"Solara," he said.

"Darian," I answered.

He took a single step in my direction.

Crack.

The sound came from above.

I broke his stare and looked up to see a massive beam—then another—detach from its joist.

Everything moved in slow motion.

Wooden rafters plummeted toward me.

Darian's mouth opened, his eyes wide with horror.

My trembling hand stretched out for his.

The sky fell and the world went dark.

24

The Aftermath

There was no light or color. I floated for a while, untethered, hollow and cold. I did not think. I did not feel. I just existed in nothingness.

Everything hurt. My skin, my bones and my brain. Every inch of me screamed.

Warm hands cradled my legs and shoulders, pulling me against something solid. A wall that trembled and throbbed like a pounding heart.

I whimpered and the heartbeat went still.

"Your Highness—"

"Get out of my way."

"There are still bombs around the building, how should we—"

"Find the Vice General. She'll handle it from here."

"But, Your Hi—"

"Get out of my way, NOW!"

Then I was moving and bouncing, each jarring impact rattling the inside of my skull.

I tried to open my eyes, but nothing happened.

Everything hurt so much.

"You're going to survive this," someone said softly. "I promise."

For some reason, I believed them. Their voice was familiar in a way that felt like more than just a memory, like something deeper and more intimately ingrained than my mind knew them. Its steady resolve soothed the limp beat of my heart, but there was something else. A tremor. A hint of fear.

"No. No. Stay with me. Open your eyes, Solara," a voice begged.

Had they closed?

"Who is she?"

"It doesn't matter. I need you to help her."

"Help her? Look at her. She doesn't need me, she needs a healer."

"Just do what you can."

"How am I supposed to—"

"Help her, Fiona. Please."

"Alright, alright. Tell me what happened."

"The Protectors attacked the Palace Armory. She went in to pull two guards from a fire. The roof caved in before she could get out."

"Blessed Gods! Why in the four realms did this woman perform a rescue mission?"

A low growl. "Because she's a damn idiot."

Silence.

"Alright. I'll just, um, go get a dress for her."

"Pants. She—she normally wears pants."

"Pants? I don't have any—never mind. I'll see what I can find. You'll stay with her until I'm back?"

More silence.

Darkness.

Light.

My eyes cracked open to a brightness so blinding that my head immediately began to spin. My body lost its sense of direction and dropped into a feeling of freefall. I clutched at the bedsheets as the world tilted and tumbled in a disorienting churn.

My fingers brushed the soft silks of a blanket. The realness of it grounded me and slowed my descent until I stopped falling and the room came into view.

I heard slow breathing and a fireplace.

My throat tightened at the first snap of a burning log. For a second, I was back inside the Palace Armory, my lungs and nose choked with putrid smoke, watching helplessly as the inferno closed in around me.

Stretching my limbs, trying to shake off the drowsiness that still clung to my senses, I noticed Darian sitting in the corner of the room in a rocking chair.

Darian's features pieced themselves back together, but they were hazy, as if the lines and angles had been smudged. I blinked rapidly, trying to clear my vision. I turned slowly. The walls were moving. Slowly, the room's color began to return.

"You're awake." Darian sat up abruptly. I waited for the frosty indifference I was so used to receiving from him, but he only frowned. "How do you feel?"

I pushed myself up and shook my head to clear my thoughts, but my brain was still mired in fog. "What happened? Where am I?"

"The Armory collapsed and you were..." He paused. "...knocked unconscious. I brought you back to the Palace to recover."

My thoughts flashed with terrifying snippets of jumbled memories. The explosions. The Protectors at the Palace Gates. The dead Royal Guards. The building engulfed in flames. Tarek—

"Tarek," I rasped, my voice breaking. Darian looked away, avoiding my gaze. I had seen the blood pooling on the Palace Gates, but I needed confirmation. A gnawing dread swirled inside me but, oddly, it did not feel as sharp as I expected. Numbness had taken hold, dulling the edges of my pain.

"And Perthe? Is he alright? And the other–"

"They're both going to be fine. Perthe was sent to Ignios to see an army healer. The other is already recovering at home."

I released a deep exhale, one I thought I might have been holding in for the entire night. At least I had managed to save a few more lives, denying The Protectors the satisfaction of taking yet another. "They made it," I murmured. "The others, the ones lying outside. Are they...?"

"A few were sent to Ignios for treatment, but most were able to return home to heal on their own. Except the woman."

I nodded in silent understanding. Her battered body was a sight I would never forget.

"Vira? Eloisa?"

"They were moved to a safe area of the Palace as soon as the bombs went off."

A long silence stretched between us.

"I'm sorry," Darian said softly, his voice tinged with empathy. "About Tarek."

He could not possibly understand how much Tarek had meant to me. How, before this mess, he had been my closest and longest-standing friend. His loss would weigh on me for the rest of my days.

Darian's hair was mussed where he had lain on it, his normally shrewd features bleary with exhaustion.

"Were you sitting there all night?" I asked.

"Yes."

"Why?"

He gave me a solemn look, but did not respond.

We sat in silence so long that the awkwardness began to grate. I huffed and shoved the blankets off. Darian stepped forward, raising a hand to stop me, but I ignored him and swung my feet over the edge of the bed, then froze.

I looked down at my body.

"Whose clothes are these?"

"Yours were destroyed. I—my cousin changed your clothes." He at least had the decency to look a little mortified. "She's a woman—my cousin, I mean. She helped you."

A glimmer of memory surfaced.

Pants. She—she normally wears pants. Not entirely true. But that was how Darian had known me.

Darian had asked his cousin to strip me down and dress me. Worse, they must have bathed me, as there was not a speck of dirt or blood left. My hair was clean and soft, falling free in brown waves. Even my nails had been scrubbed and filed into a delicate arch.

I was, indeed, wearing pants. Sleek and darkest blue, made of some thick and stretchy fabric I had never worn before, with hardened armor sewn into the thighs and hips. It reminded me of the Royal Guard's uniform.

"Are you still hurt?"

My gaze snapped back up. "Hurt?"

"It was difficult to tell if your injuries were serious. I had planned to call for a healer when you woke up."

I frowned. "Injuries?"

I flexed each of my limbs, pushed up my sleeves to examine my arms and ran my fingers along my neck and face. No swelling, no cuts, no bruises. Other than some soreness and a lingering stiff neck, I felt no worse than after a night of hard drinking.

"I... I think I'm fine. I made it through the night, so probably nothing internal. "I tried to muster a good-natured scowl, though it felt forced. "You shouldn't wait to call for a healer for a Haren, you know. We aren't like you Aquara. Our bodies don't always heal just because we're still breathing."

He gave me a strange look. "You don't really believe that, do you?"

"Believe what?"

"That you're not..."

A furious buzzing filled my head, a war of whispers and memories, questions and accusations colliding all at once.

My feet shuffled awkwardly. "I should get home. My father must be out roaming the streets looking for me by now."

"I sent a message to your family."

I stood. "You did what?"

"I suspected they would be concerned if you did not return, so I spoke with the Palace Courier. He said he was familiar with your family. I had him send them a message saying that you were safe and staying here for the night."

I did not want to imagine what Kian would do when he found out Tarek was dead. He would shut himself away from the world, probably in his room, curtains drawn, unreachable.

I tried to distract myself from the emptiness I felt inside, but every time I closed my eyes, Tarek's face flickered behind my eyelids. His laughter under the Sun, the warmth of his presence at the tavern on weekends and the way he had always been my anchor in the storm. Now, all that was left was a hollow ache and a relentless reminder of what we had lost.

Tarek was too full of hope for a world that had no place for him. It was so easy to see now how The Protectors' violent methods had swallowed him whole. He had wanted to make a real difference, but he got caught up in a system that resorted to burning everything to the ground. He dreamt of a world where leaders ruled with integrity and foresight, where resources were shared fairly and peace was a tangible reality, but, in the end, his vision clashed with a system that refused to bend.

Now, with Darian the most likely heir to the throne, the fragile future of Aetherium and Aquara's uneasy ties to its three neighboring regions hung on the weight of his choices.

"So," I teased lightly, though the tension coiling in my stomach betrayed me, "what is Prince Darian going to do now?"

"The Council is meeting," he said finally, his voice low but steady. "They'll decide what comes next."

The ground seemed to shift beneath me as it all came rushing back. The King had not survived, and the Palace had been cloaked in a somber hush ever since. I had been the last to see him alive, to witness his final breaths. It was almost certain now that Darian would be chosen to take the throne.

Darian's presence should have been daunting. He was now the most powerful person in the realm, yet something about him felt oddly familiar. We had shared too many moments for the formality of kinship to erase the acquaintance we shared.

The room seemed to close in around us as I struggled to regain my composure. The silence stretched.

His tone turned serious. "We need to talk."

"What's so urgent?" I asked, though I had a sinking feeling about where this conversation was going.

Darian took a deep breath, his eyes searching mine with a mix of intensity and something else that looked like desperation. "It's about your mother."

My heart skipped a beat. I had been meaning to ask him about my mother for a long time.

"What about her?" I asked, trying to keep my voice steady.

"There's something you need to know." Darian's tone was grave. "She's been working with me. Or rather, she was. Before—" He stopped, struggling to find the right words.

I leaned in closer, my curiosity piqued. "Before what?"

"Before the attack," Darian said slowly, his tone nearly a whisper. "She was involved in something important. She gave me something—"

"What?" The single word escaped my lips with forceful urgency.

"What have you heard about Emberberry?" Darian asked.

My jaw slackened in shock. A cold chill raced down my spine. Emberberry. The name conjured memories of hushed conversations and hidden jars. I had grown up forcing the bitter purple berries down my throat every morning, used to the dull feverish haze they coated over everything. The same berry that was locked behind a gilded cabinet in the Palace Apothecary that Vira had shown me.

My voice cracked. "It's rare. It needs purified water."

Darian nodded. "Exactly. Water purer than anything found in Aquara. And your mother found it."

The world tilted. "Found…what?"

"In the desert. A source so pure it could sustain the Emberberry."

My breath caught. My mother. Working with Darian. All those nights she slipped away from home. The quiet smiles when I pressed her for answers. The shattered jar in our hearth. I wondered how she would feel if she knew this moment had come.

I frowned. "Why is the Emberberry so important to Aquara?"

"It's not…" Darian hesitated, then swallowed. "It's important to the King"

I narrowed my eyes. "The King?"

He swallowed again. "He…he had his own ways of…hearing voices. Seeing visions. The Emberberry helped him control it. Your mother and I were the only people who knew about this."

The voices—even the King could not escape them. It finally made sense why the King's Emberberry was so closely guarded.

"What were you and my mother arguing about that day in Paradise Row?" The realization dawned. "'Is that why she left?'"

"We had reached an agreement," Darian said quietly. "She would supply Emberberry for the King but on two conditions: first, that the water source would remain secret. Second, that Liora would be allowed to provide it to others in Haren. In return, Liora agreed to keep the King's condition a secret and to maintain an uninterrupted supply of Emberberry."

My head tilted. "Why did she disappear?"

"The King reconsidered the agreement and offered to share the water source equally across the four regions of Aetherium if your mother was prepared to reveal its location. Liora was the only person who could interpret the ancient Haren maps that revealed its location—"

I connected the dots, finishing for him. "—so my mother refused the King's offer because she did not trust him. And she went into hiding to save her life."

It all made sense. Finally.

I swallowed hard, my throat tight. "Why are you only telling me this now?" I whispered.

"Because you deserve to know," he said simply. Then, softer, almost pleading, "And because I need you to trust me. Without you, without what your mother passed to you, we can't finish what she began."

"Where is she?" I asked, my voice barely audible.

"Somewhere in the Haren desert."

The Haren Desert. I had once approached its edge on a school trip, where guides told tales of travelers lost to the endless dunes and caravans swallowed whole in merciless sandstorms. During the day, the Sun turned the sand into a burning ocean. At night, the cold was just as deadly. If the temperatures did not claim you, the sand itself would, whipping against skin and leaving a patchwork of red and freckled marks. The merchants who crossed it often bore faded grazes along their arms, earned in days spent in relentless wind and grit.

If my mother had ever entered that desert and *stayed*… it was not for adventure or wealth. She did it because she truly believed in the work.

"As you know," Darian continued, his tone lower now, "she hasn't returned in months. Which means Liora's found the water source. At this point, she's likely cultivated a small crop of Emberberry. The Blood Sun from a few months ago must have helped her seedlings survive."

"How do we get to her?"

"Well…" He hesitated, chewing on his words like he was not sure how much to give. "The night before she disappeared, she was scouring a map. I'm sure she saw something."

Of course. Second only to her gift for healing, my mother had an extraordinary talent with maps. She could take a vague sketch of a winding trail or a scattered settlement and turn it into a work of precision, adding hidden markers or warnings only someone with her eyes could understand. Many of the maps in our stash were hers: traced, redrawn, improved and annotated with cryptic symbols that made sense only to her.

Darian looked at me then, like he was asking something.

"You need a Hawkthorne to look at it," I paused. "You need me."

Darian and I walked through the Palace's winding stairways and narrow halls. I stayed quickly on his tail, afraid to lose him and the secrets he had finally shared with me.

As we ascended, passing a few servants who quickly averted their gazes, a strange dread settled over me. Why was everyone avoiding our stare? My cheeks were damp with tears, the salty tracks stinging in the cool air. I could not stop thinking of the last few hours. The bombing. My mother. Tarek. I felt a heavy weight in my chest and had to swallow hard to keep the sobs at bay.

How could this be true? My mother, beloved healer of Haren, had been conspiring with Darian all this time and I had not had the faintest clue. The only clue had been that note I had stumbled upon weeks ago, tucked among her maps.

She had always loved maps. I remembered countless nights when her silhouette was barely visible in the dim flicker of candlelight. Hunched over her desk, she traced the ridges and valleys with the precision of a cartographer. She would draw for hours with steady hands and intent eyes. I had thought it was nothing more than a harmless obsession. Now, Darian's words echoed: *There's no one quite like Liora.*

We reached a narrow tower stairwell. Darian stopped suddenly, snapping me out of my thoughts. He pressed a hand to the tower wall, fingers sliding over the damp stone. We were close to the top—thin blades of moonlight cut through narrow windows, washing everything in ghostly light. The silence pressed in, heavy, suffocating.

"What in the Gods' name—"

"Shh." His hiss cut through the stillness.

I swallowed my words, watching as his hand swept the wall with maddening patience. My pulse quickened. Then his fingers froze. A flicker of triumph appeared at the corner of his mouth as he pushed against a crack in the stone.

CLICK.

The sound echoed down the stairwell. My breath caught as part of the wall groaned and shifted, revealing a narrow hidden door. Its edges were so well concealed in the stone that I wondered how many had passed by it without ever knowing.

Darian shoved it open. The hinges screamed with age, and darkness loomed beyond. He stepped inside without hesitation, flicking a switch. Pale light spilled into a narrow corridor, shadows writhing along the walls.

I lingered at the threshold, every instinct warning me to turn back. Darian glanced over his shoulder, catching my hesitation.

"Coming?" he asked calmly.

"Yes. I trust you," I said quietly.

"You don't have to trust me. Just trust that the answers are in here."

I hesitated for a beat longer before finally stepping inside. The weight of my doubts pressed down on me. Had Darian ever brought my mother here? Had she walked these very halls?

The door creaked as Darian shut it behind us, the heavy click of the lock echoing through the confined space like a judge's gavel. The sound made our isolation all too real.

"Years ago, when the Aquara Elder built this Palace, he created hidden rooms for sanctuary in case the Palace was ever under attack," Darian began. "Today, hardly anyone knows they exist."

My eyes adjusted to the dim light as I took in our surroundings. The hallway, narrow and lined with smooth stone, led us to a small chamber at the end. It was an intimate space, barely large enough to fit more than a handful of people. In the center stood a sturdy wooden table, its surface scarred by time and illuminated by a single brass lamp that hung from the low ceiling above it.

The walls were lined with shelves, each one meticulously arranged with items that spoke of both history and secrecy. There were dusty tomes with cracked spines, their titles worn and faded, along with jars filled with curious, unidentifiable substances. Ancient relics, small statues and strange artifacts were tucked between stacks of parchment and rolled-up scrolls. One shelf held a collection of intricate glass bottles, their contents shimmering with colors I could not name. The air was thick with the scent of old paper and something else, something earthy, like damp stone after a rainstorm.

We were alone in the hidden depths of the Palace. There were no windows, only the walls and the shelves and the oppressive sense of being completely sealed off from the outside world. I approached the table, the faint creak of the floorboards the only sound in the stillness. My eyes were drawn to the maps spread across its surface. They were detailed, showing the entire region of Aetherium, with every mountain, dune and hidden trail painstakingly marked. Some were old, their edges frayed, while others looked freshly drawn, the ink still sharp and vivid.

"Vira and I used to come here to play hide and seek when we were little," Darian said, a faint smile touching his lips as he ran his fingers over one of the maps.

"Princess Vira? Does she kno—?" I asked, my curiosity piqued, wondering just how much of his partnership with my mother he had revealed to her.

"She knows little of this," he replied, his tone suddenly more guarded. "It's for her own good."

I nodded. I had my own share of hidden truths. I had kept my encounter with Emberberry at the Palace secret from Kian, along with all the other strange events that had happened since I took over my mother's duties at the Palace. I spared him the details and weight of it all. I thought of him now, probably brooding and jealous of the sleep I had supposedly been getting all this time in Aquara's finest sheets.

Darian's attention shifted back to the maps. "Your mother and I worked many days here. We made quite a bit of progress." He gestured to the table.

I imagined my mother spending her time here, with Darian's pencil behind her ear and her slender fingers tracing the map. While she was supposedly on Palace Healer duty, she had actually been here in this stuffy room, helping Darian.

"This was the one she kept looking at," Darian said, shaking me out of my thoughts. He laid the map out on the table.

I studied it intently, letting my eyes wander over the detailed illustrations of Aetherium. Each map depicted a different region.

Ignios, the smoldering volcanoes to the west, their peaks drawn with jagged lines. Terra, the vast plains stretching out to the south, rendered with sweeping strokes that suggested the endless expanse of grasslands and the rolling winds that danced across them. Aquara, with its spired Palace at the heart of the capital, sprawled along intricate waterways that fanned outward like veins of liquid silver. Even Haren's Technology District seemed alive, its factories puffing clouds of smoke as if breathing.

It was the northern region that drew my attention. The lines there were more intricate, more complex. My eyes followed the curves and angles until they landed on a small and almost imperceptible phrase written in ancient script. The letters were delicate and barely legible against the faded parchment.

Darian's finger traced the lines, stopping at that very phrase. "Find me at the North of all Norths," he translated, his voice dropping to a whisper that sent a shiver down my spine. The phrase was signed with a small dash and the letter "L." My stomach knotted. It could not be.

It was a message from my mother.

We spread the maps across the table, studying them in silence. Slowly, a troubling realization sank in: each map had a different north. None of them lined up the way they should. Rivers curved in impossible directions, ridges slanted at odd angles, dunes twisted in spirals that did not match. How could something so fundamental be so wrong?

I pressed my hands flat on the paper, tilting and nudging the maps against each other. At first, nothing fit. Then, as my eyes sharpened, I noticed patterns beginning to emerge: a bend in a river on one map aligned with a ridge on another. A dune spiral, rotated just so, threaded perfectly into its counterpart. My pulse quickened.

"They all point to the same place," I whispered, my voice barely audible. "The water source. That's where she is."

Layer by layer, we matched rivers to ridges and dunes to valleys. The lines converged, slicing across the maps, intersecting at one precise spot. My heart hammered against my ribs.

Darian leaned closer, his brow furrowed. "Could that... really be it?" he murmured, almost to himself.

To be certain, we grabbed the historical dune maps. Paper after paper, the sands shifted wildly across the years, dancing with every gust. One place never moved. One fixed point in a sea of endless motion. Water does not shift like sand.

I held my breath, tracing the spot with a trembling finger. "This is it. This is where she is."

Darian shook his head, a thin smile of awe tugging at his lips. "She knew we'd find it if we just paid attention."

25

The Council

The dim Council Chamber was lit only by the flickering glow of torches mounted on the stone walls. The room was a square, two levels below ground, with bare stone on the walls, floor and ceiling. The austere design of the room was intended to evoke a sense of solemn tradition with no distractions, only the constant reminder of the absolute power of the King and his Council.

As the robed members of King Thalor's Council shuffled into the room, shadows danced across the long oak table at its center.

At the head of the table sat Lord Ferrick, the Lord Chancellor, a wiry man with hawkish features and eyes that glinted like steel. When all twelve members of the King's Council were finally seated, Lord Ferrick rapped his knuckles on the wood to silence the murmurs that rippled through the room.

"The King is dead," his voice boomed. "Our first order is to ensure a smooth transition. Prince Darian will assume the throne."

A chorus of protests erupted but none were louder than Lady Maris, the High Stewardess, her copper hair catching the firelight. "Darian? That spoiled princeling? He's weak and liberal in his thoughts! He'll bring this Kingdom to ashes." It was not unusual for the Council, in the absence of their King, to speak with such brazen candor. They were far more respectful whenever discussing any one of the twelve in their cabal.

Ferrick's gaze swept the room, daring anyone else to challenge him. "We have no choice. Prince Darian is Thalor's blood. His ascension is law."

Lord Constantine, Lord of Military Affairs despite never having served, added, "It may be in the Kingdom's favor to have a weak Prince Darian as King if he wields the power of this Council's wisdom. I do worry, however, that he might still go rogue with his misguided ideas."

Lord Venn, the Lord of the Treasury, a portly man with a voice like gravel, leaned forward, "Laws can be amended. Perhaps the Council should retain power until Prince Darian proves he can be controlled."

A chorus of eyes began to follow Lord Venn's suggestion with interest, but the debate was cut short when a guard in full armor burst through the heavy oak doors. He saluted hastily.

"My Lords, My Lady. Lord Ferrick, urgent news from the Capital! The Aquara water supply has been poisoned. Blotchbane."

The room fell silent. Even Lady Maris's perpetual scowl turned to shock. "Blotchbane? That's not possible," she whispered. "The only known source is..."

"Haren," Lord Ferrick finished grimly. He turned to the guard. "What's the scope?"

"Hospitals are overflowing. Terras are very ill but mostly surviving. Ignios complain of stomach issues, but Aquaras—"

"Are dying," Lord Ferrick said, his voice like stone.

The guard nodded. "The contamination started three days ago, my Lord. They hit all of the main reservoirs and all but one of the reserve emergency ones. We have only three days' supply of safe water left for Aquara."

Lord Ferrick's racing mind was connecting fragments of information. "The bombings were a distraction."

Lady Maris slammed her palm on the table. "Haren. It's always them! We should march on their lands and finish off every last one of them."

"Revenge can wait," Lord Venn interjected, his face pale. "If Aquara's water is poisoned, the people must be warned. We must also immediately lock down the remaining safe reservoirs."

"Do it," Lord Ferrick barked to the guard. "Send riders right now. No one drinks the tainted water. Post edicts in every square."

"And what of the sick?" Lady Maris's voice wavered for the first time. "If the hospitals are full…"

"Then the healers will have to ration their aid," Lord Ferrick said harshly. "We don't have the resources to save everyone.'

A new voice chimed in. It was Lord Kael, the Master of the Intelligence Unit, who had been quiet until now. His golden hair framed his aristocratic face.

"Terra is faring well. They could try to rise to dominance amidst this chaos."

"A temporary dominance," Lady Maris shot back. "The Terra are irrelevant. Simple peasants. They lack leadership and will bicker among themselves before long."

Lord Ferrick's fist slammed onto the table. "Enough! Our priority is containing this disaster. Haren's actions cannot go unanswered, but retaliation now risks further destabilization. As for Prince Darian, we'll invoke the Council's extra powers. If he fails to act, we won't."

A silence followed that was heavy with unspoken fears. Then another guard entered, his face pale. "My Lords, my Lady. News from the healers. Haren are completely immune. They have ingested the antidote to Blotchbane from drinking contaminated water much of their lives. The water poisoning was deliberate."

The room erupted in voices again, clashing in a cacophony of rage and despair.

"The Haren will pay for this," Lord Kael muttered. "There will be justice."

Lady Maris stood, her voice cutting through the din. "Justice will come, but first, survival."

Lord Ferrick's steely gaze met hers and he nodded. "Three days. That's all we have to stop this madness."

"Where is Prince Darian?"

26

The Desert

As Darian and I slipped through the Palace Gates, the air was thick with the faint scent of jasmine from the Royal Gardens we left behind. Our hoods were pulled low, shadows cloaking our faces, and our satchels hung heavy against our sides, packed with three days' worth of carefullyrationed food. The calculations had been meticulous: from the imposing Aquara Palace to the coordinates etched in the far reaches of the Haren desert. Stealing a Sand Skimmer had briefly crossed our minds. The sleek vehicle would have cut the journey to mere hours, but the Royal Guard would have tracked us down before the dust even settled. On foot, we were untraceable.

With the Palace a safe distance behind us, I became aware of my stomach clenching with hunger. It was a feeling I had learned to ignore, but when Darian reached into his satchel and pulled out a loaf of soft bread and a pair of oranges stolen from the Royal Kitchens, the sight alone made my throat tighten. Blessed Sun God, my mouth flooded with saliva. I forced myself to look away, clenching my jaw against the hunger gnawing at me, but my stomach betrayed me with a growl.

Darian shot me a sideways grin. "Hungry already?" he teased, holding the bread just out of reach.

I glared at him. "Put it away, Darian. We have rations for a reason."

"And oranges don't count as rations?" he quipped, tearing a piece of bread and tossing it in his mouth with a dramatic flourish.

"Not if you eat them all on the first night," I snapped, my voice low and sharp.

Before fleeing the Royal Palace, I had one last solemn duty to fulfill. I left a letter for Kian and father, a carefully crafted lie about staying at the Palace to tend to the wounded after the bombings. Tarek's name was conspicuously absent. I could not bear to write it down. I wanted so much to believe that, when I returned to Sand City, he would be there. I imagined an alternate reality in which he would be leaning against the wall with that familiar smirk, ready to tease me about my endless duties or drag me to the tavern for one last drink, but I had to face that this part of my life was over. Tarek was gone and no amount of denial could bring him back.

The Protectors. My thoughts turned to them as we walked farther toward the outskirts of Nereidia. Had they considered the bombing a victory? What had they done with Tarek? Had they even given him the decency of a burial? I believed in their cause for justice and equality, but bombs would not win this fight. The Aquara crushed the riot before it even began. The bombing was no more than a minor nuisance for the Aquara, which would be easily erased. Yet The Protectors paid with their lives.

My father's words echoed in my mind. *Desperation is the ultimate motivator. People will go to unspeakable lengths to cling to hope when all else seems lost.* The Protectors were no different, gathering the desperate and the hopeless under their banner.

My mind wandered to Rhea, the woman who had once been like an aunt to me, with her teasing smiles and voice of quiet wisdom. How could she lead such a group? How could a woman so wise condone the sacrifice of so many young lives?

Princess Vira's face, marred with Blotchbane scars, flashed in my mind and my stomach churned. Rhea had allowed this. She had sanctioned it. Tarek had never wanted this. I had to believe that. His dream had been of fairness and reform—yet he had stormed the Palace Gates, planted those bombs, killed Royal Guardsmen.

Finding the Emberberry and my mother was not just about survival. It was a promise to Tarek and his dream of equality. The least I could do was try to honor that.

The farther Darian and I walked into the desert night, the colder the air grew. Erratic gusts of wind penetrated our layers of clothing. I pulled my hood tighter, wrapping it over my shoulders as I rubbed my arms for warmth. The sand blowing across my face was restless and biting, like pinpricks on my skin.

It was me who spoke first.

"Darian," I whispered, my voice barely audible over the faint rustle of sand. "Are you sure this is the right way? The compass has been pointing the same direction for hours."

He did not respond immediately, his eyes fixed on the horizon as if searching for some sign in the darkness. When he finally spoke, his voice was laced with uncertainty. "The desert plays tricks on the mind. It's easy to doubt, to second-guess every step, but the stars don't lie. We're heading true. We have to trust that."

Trust. The word felt fragile. Trusting the compass, trusting the stars and trusting the thin scraps of parchment that bore the weight of everything we were risking. What else could we do? Doubt was a luxury we could not afford. I nodded, though the motion was more for my benefit than his.

The moon hung high when we stopped to rest. We chose a spot near a lone shrub. At least here the ground was more mud than the fine sand that had been swirling around us for hours, lodging itself into the cracks of my sandals and the tangles of my hair.

Darian unrolled the mat with deliberate movements that were careful and practiced. As he laid down, I caught the glint of steel daggers he had unsheathed and set within arm's reach.

"We're close," he said, his voice a quiet rasp against the night. "Maybe six kilometers east. She should be there."

His certainty felt hollow, but I nodded anyway, murmuring an agreement that neither of us believed.

The breeze picked up again, brushed over my arms and sent another shiver down my spine. I curled tighter under my hood. The cold was not what gnawed at me as much as it was the stillness. Lying there left me vulnerable to my own thoughts racing out of control.

I thought of the King. His dying breath. The way his clouded and failing eyes had locked onto mine with a strange intensity. *My daughter,* he had whispered, the words thick with finality. I lay there, thinking. Had Darian heard the King's final whisper? Surely not.

It could not have been real. A fevered delusion. The last ramblings of an unraveling mind. King Thalor did not have a daughter. Everyone knew that.

Fight.

The familiar word throbbed in my skull like a drumbeat. I clenched my jaw and squeezed my eyes shut, but it did not help. The words felt like a splinter lodged deep in my chest. It could not be true. They were not true.

"Why?" The question tore from me before I could stop it.

Beside me, Darian shifted, his silhouette outlined faintly by the silver light of the moon. For a moment, I thought he might feign sleep, but then he answered, his voice low and measured.

"What do you mean?"

I propped myself up on one elbow and the coarse fibers of the mat scratched my skin. "This," I gestured vaguely at the endless expanse of desert stretching around us, the cracked, dry shrub barely clinging to life beside us and the satchels of stolen provisions sitting heavy. "Why are you here? Why are you risking everything for this mission?"

He was silent for a moment, his gaze fixed on the stars above us. The silver light cast a sharp silhouette of his face, but his expression was unreadable. Finally, he exhaled.

"Because I have no choice," he said.

His words were simple, but his tone was not. There was something bitter in it, something that pulled taut between us like a thread about to unravel before snapping.

"You *do* have a choice," I said, frowning. "You could've stayed in the Palace. You could've stayed safe. "

Darian turned his head slightly and his eyes met mine for the briefest of moments before looking away to the sky. His lips pressed into a thin line.

"You think I was safe there?" he said quietly, almost to himself. "Do you think I didn't see it? What my uncle was doing? What he was building? Every banquet, every Council meeting and every time he handed down some edict meant to tighten his grip on the regions—I was there. I watched him carve this Kingdom into pieces, and I said nothing."

His voice cracked on the last word and he looked away, his jaw tightening.

I did not know what to say.

Darian let out a low and humorless laugh. "I was nine when I realized that the power wasn't meant for everyone. My uncle told the Court it was for the good of the people and to maintain order. Later that night, I heard him laughing with his advisors, saying that it wasn't for the people at all. It was for control. He often said, 'Those who hold the power shall rule the realms.'"

His fists clenched at his sides and his knuckles whitened. "He never cared about the people, not really. I was too much of a coward to stop him."

"You were just a child," I said, my voice softer now.

"And I grew up," he snapped, his eyes blazing as they finally met mine. "I grew up and I stayed silent. For years I stayed silent, because I thought 'what difference would it make?' I thought I could fix it later, but now there's no 'later.' If I don't act now, everything he hoarded will fall into the wrong hands."

He broke off, breathing hard, his hands shaking slightly.

"Wrong hands?" I asked, softer this time.

Darian did not look at me. "You don't get it, do you?"

"Get what?"

He turned towards me, his expression taut with something raw. "That Palace? Those titles? They mean nothing. I'm the Prince, Solara, but I have no real power. None of it was ever mine."

I blinked, caught off guard by the intensity in his voice. "You're the heir to the throne, Darian. If anyone has power, it's you."

Darian let out another hollow laugh. The bitter tone in his voice returned. "The throne is a cage, not a crown. Everything I'm supposed to inherit has already been stripped bare, sold off, or weaponized. My uncle made sure of that. The water, the people and the regions, they're just pieces on a board he's spent decades arranging. When he was done with them, he arranged me as well."

"What do you mean?" I asked, my voice hesitant.

He sat up slightly, his knees drawn to his chest, and raked a hand through his hair. "Do you know what it's like to be groomed for something you don't even want? To be told you'll inherit a Kingdom, but only as long as you follow the rules someone else wrote? Every step, every word and every decision predetermined and controlled. I don't get to rule, Solara. I get to obey."

I frowned, my heart sinking at the frustration etched across his face. "But you could change things. If you're King—"

"I'll never be King," he interrupted, his tone sharp. "Not the way you're thinking. The Council already decided that years ago. If I don't toe the line, they'll find someone else. They don't need me, they need a puppet."

"Then why leave?" I asked, my voice rising slightly. "If you don't have power, if you're just a pawn to them, why risk everything to be here? Why put yourself in the middle of all this?"

His jaw clenched, and for a moment, I thought he would not answer. Then he exhaled and the tension in his shoulders eased just slightly.

"Because even a pawn can ruin the board if it's played right," he said, his voice low. "My uncle's death created a fracture the Council is scrambling to fix. They view me as a liability now, that's too unpredictable to control and they're right. I might not have power in the Palace, but out here…" He gestured to the desert around us and his expression hardened. "Out here, I can choose what to fight for. I can choose what to destroy."

His words settled heavily in the air between us, carrying an edge of defiance that made my chest tighten. I stared at him and the weight of his words sank deep into my chest. He had never been so up-front with me. "Darian…"

He shook his head, laid back down and turned away from me. "Go to sleep, Solara. We have a long way to go tomorrow."

I lay back down slowly and pulled my hood tighter against the chill. It was in those few minutes, lying on the desert sand, that I think I finally understood Darian.

27

The Water

THREE DAYS LATER

The morning sun hung in the sky like a molten eye, looking down on us. Its heat pressed down relentlessly. Every breath was exhausting. The horizon shimmered with undulating waves of sand, mocking us with promises of water that did not exist.

It had been almost three days since either of us had eaten or drunk anything. The water satchels had been empty since the first night, drained faster than either of us wanted to admit. Now, my mouth felt like a dry cavern of dust.

I staggered ahead of Darian with an uneven gait. We did not talk anymore—words required energy we did not have. What was there to say? His labored breaths behind me spoke volumes. His skin was pale, sickly and taut. His steps faltered more with each passing hour.

Suddenly, Darian stumbled and fell to his knees. A light groan escaped him. I did not stop. I did not even look back.

"Wait," he croaked, his voice barely audible.

I slowed but did not turn around.

"You have to get up," I said, my voice hoarse.

"I can't," he whispered. His hands dug into the sand, the grains sifting through his fingers. "I can't do this anymore."

"Yes, you can."

"No, I can't!" The words erupted from him, raw and jagged. "I'm done, Solara! I can't—" His voice cracked, and his shoulders shook. Hot tears pricked his eyes. "I can't keep walking towards nothing."

I turned then, my face shadowed by the sun but my eyes blazing. "If you give up now, you're giving up on more than yourself. What about the Council? Don't you want to get there first?"

"Don't," he said, his voice shaking. "Don't put that on me. Don't talk to me about duty or purpose or whatever righteous cause you think we're serving out here. This isn't noble, Solara. It's death."

"Maybe it is," I said in a low voice. "But if we die out here, at least we tried. At least we didn't just let them win."

He laughed bitterly, the sound grating against the stillness. "Who's *them*? The Council? The Protectors? The whole damn world? They've already won, Solara. Look at us!"

I did not answer. I just stared at his chest as I noticed that his breathing was becoming irregular. Slowly, I crouched beside him, eyes locked on the nape of his neck. A faint red swirl was blooming there, spiraling like an ink stain under his skin. I reached out, and my fingers trembled as they traced the mark. It was warm to the touch, like a dying ember. I knew it instantly. The same pattern had covered Princess Vira's skin before she succumbed.

Blotchbane. Poison.

"You've been poisoned," I murmured.

Fight.

"What?" His voice wavered, eyes wide and wild. "Poisoned? How— when—?"

"Hush." I cut him off, my tone sharp.

Fight.

Hovering my hand above his skin, I closed my eyes. A tingling heat spread through me and rushed like a flood into every crevice of my being. It was unbearable, like shards of ice melting into fire, searing my every nerve. My breathing hitched as I felt the poison, the venomous tendrils snaking through his bloodstream, coiling tighter around his life.

When I opened my eyes, the red swirls were gone, replaced by faint scars and pale traces of veins beneath his skin.

Darian stared at me, his lips parted in disbelief. "That was incredible… you have it, don't you?"

"What?"

"The… the light. The powers."

"Yes," I said quietly, avoiding his gaze. It was unavoidable.

"I knew it," he murmured, wonder and fear tangled in his tone. Then he hushed, almost to himself. "Just like Uncle."

"Why did you not—"

"I tried to, but couldn't save him. I don't control it. It controls me."

"And the Emberberry?"

"Yes. If I don't eat…" My voice faded mid-sentence. I did not wish to hear myself say it.

"What happens when you don't eat it?" His question hung in the air like a noose.

"Then the noises and the voices get louder. The visions get stronger," I said, my voice barely above a whisper.

Darian's breath stopped for a second, but he did not say anything. He just looked at me.

"Let's go," I said, standing and pulling him up. My legs trembled under the effort, but I did not let go. "We're not dying out here."

This time, he followed.

We knew we had reached the North of all Norths when the endless desert broke right up against a rocky cliffside that rose several hundred feet above us. As we approached the cliff, we recognised the letter 'L' emblazoned in black, taking up the entire height of the cliff. There, below the 'L', was the jagged mouth of the cave. The opening loomed wide enough to swallow a caravan whole, its teeth of black stone rising nearly thirty feet high.

The air shifted the moment we stepped inside. The dry, blistering breath of the desert gave way to a damp coolness that clung to the skin. Our footsteps no longer sank into sand, but crunched against scattered stones.

And then I saw it.

Nestled in a shallow hollow of the cavern floor lay a glimmering pool of water—no more than a few feet across, but radiant with life. The surface was so still it looked like polished glass, reflecting flecks of light from the cave's mineral walls. Around its edges, thin shoots stretched upward, pale green stalks climbing higher than my waist. From them hung clusters of swollen, purple globes that pulsed with a faint inner glow. Their light painted the cave walls in gentle violet hues.

Emberberries. My tongue remembered their taste before my mind did: sharp bitterness that curled into sweetness at the back of the throat. I remembered the taste, thick and acrid, sliding down my throat, muting the visions until only silence remained.

"She did it," Darian breathed beside me.

I had never seen them like this. Never more than a handful at a time. And yet here they were, alive, glowing and impossibly abundant. Dozens of them, ripe and heavy, bowing the long shoots toward the pool. The air was perfumed faintly with their tang, a fragrance that brought back every morning I had crushed them beneath a stone, every night I had sipped their faint, bitter brew.

The water was clearer than any I had ever seen. Not the brackish rations doled from clay, not the clouded trickle stolen from canals. This was water that seemed to breathe, its surface glimmering like crystal. My throat convulsed at the sight. My knees nearly buckled with the urge to fall forward and drink, to press my face against the surface and drown myself in relief.

I had taken a step, already leaning toward the pool, when a sound froze me in place.

A soft, lilting voice. My name.

"Solara."

It echoed across the cavern, gentle but undeniable.

My breath caught in my chest.

"Did you hear that?" I asked, my voice hoarse from days of thirst and disuse.

Darian's head snapped up. His eyes swept the cavern walls as he gave the smallest nod.

Then the voice again—faint but unmistakable.

"Solara."

My breath hitched. It was my name.

I did not answer. My legs moved before my mind could catch up, dragging me toward the sound.

"Solara," the voice called again, louder and clearer now.

Then I saw her.

She emerged from behind a jagged outcrop of stone, her figure limned by the faint violet glow of the berries. My breath snagged hard in my chest. For an instant, my mind refused to accept what I was seeing.

It was her.

I stopped dead in my tracks.

"Mother?" The word barely escaped me.

Her lips curved into a smile. Her face was thinner than I remembered and her once-dark hair was streaked with gray. But it was her.

Her smile trembled. "It's me, Solara."

The world tilted. The relentless heat of the desert disappeared. My legs wobbled, but I locked my knees and refused to fall.

"No," I said, the word tumbling out before I could stop it. "No. You're not real. You can't be real."

Her smile faltered. She took a step closer, her hands trembling at her sides. "It's me," she said. "It's really me."

Darian caught up to me then. His shadow fell over mine. He looked directly at my mother. "Liora!"

I ignored him, my eyes locked on her. "You left," I said, my voice cracking. "You left us. You left me."

Her face crumpled and tears welled in her eyes. "I know," she whispered. "I know I did."

"You," I spat, my voice trembling with the force of emotions I had held back for months. "You left without a word. We did not know if you were alive or dead."

Her expression did not falter, though tears shone in her eyes. "I did it for you, Solara," she said softly. "I did not tell anyone because I needed to protect you. If they interrogated you and if you knew where I was, it would have put you in danger."

"Danger?" I repeated, my voice rising. "We were already in danger! Every single day without you was hell and you just… you just disappeared."

"I was trying to save you," she insisted, stepping closer. "And Kian. It was the only way to keep you safe."

The anger surged again, but before I could unleash it she gestured behind her. "Let me show you."

We followed my mother down a narrow path that seemed to dead-end at the cave wall. As we reached the wall, the path made a sharp turn and kept going. We could now see sunlight streaming in through a second opening at the far end of the path. I realised then: this was not just a cave, it was a tunnel that cut clean through the cliff.

When we reached the opening and stepped out into the light, I froze. The view was breathtaking, even more spectacular than the view of the gardens from the Palace balcony. Spread before us was a vast crater lake, its water glinting silver-blue under the sun. Jagged rock walls rose hundreds of feet around it, cradling a precious body of water spanning several miles across. The water was crystal-clear all the way to its sandy floor.

Darian let out a sharp breath beside me. Neither of us could speak.

My mother knelt at the edge and cupped her hands, drinking deeply. Then she turned back to us, calm, proud, as though she had been waiting for this moment for years.

"Try it," she said. "This is the purest water in Aetherium. At its heart, the lake plunges thousands of feet deep. The cave and the lake are both fed by an underground aquifer. Enough to sustain all of Aetherium for generations."

I could not resist. "Unless the Aquara drain it dry for their fountains."

She gave me a wry smile, but said nothing. "Come," she said, leading us along the cliff path skirting the water.

I knew instantly, from the restrained excitement in the way she said "come", that she was savouring the moment before a big reveal.

But the path remained steep, with loose gravel slipping beneath our soles forcing us to keep our gaze pinned to the ground.

As the path leveled out, we came upon another breathtaking view. Before us stretched a terraced grove, a sea of violet and amethyst Emberberry. Lantern-like fruit glimmered like a constellation, each spring-green stalk heavy with dozens of silky berries. They seemed to hold fragments of the sun and burned with a quiet glow, even in daylight. I understood why they were called the Emberberry.

"These are the only seeds in Aetherium," my mother said softly. "They exist nowhere else. They drink only the purest water—water this realm hasn't seen in generations. That's why I had to find this place. I had to hide it from the Guards along the Haren border. Why I had to protect it."

I reached out and brushed one with my finger. It felt cool, silk-thin. So delicate, as if it might dissolve at my touch. To see them in a jar at home had been one thing. To see them alive like this was another.

"As long as they stay in darkness after harvest, they'll last for a year," she said. "But here, in the light, they thrive. They are pure. Like life itself."

I gazed over the terraces, each glowing with sacred lanterns, and realized this was no ordinary crop. It was a treasure.

Every decision, every sacrifice… was for this. For you." Her hands trembled as she turned to me. "So Darian could protect his uncle. And so you could survive."

I stared at her, confused.

"You both carry The Light," she said.

Her gaze fixed on me, steady, unflinching.

Devourer of Crowns. Ravager of Vengeance. My daughter.

The words crashed over me. I had suspected, but this was the confirmation I had longed for. He *was* my father.

Endless questions tore through me, each heavier than the last. The anger I had clung to for so long wanted to flare again. But in her eyes, I saw love and guilt braided together.

"I'm sorry," she whispered. "I never stopped loving you. Never."

I hesitated, then gave in, falling into her arms. The anger dissolved into something warmer, fragile but real. For the first time in years, I felt whole.

"I love you," I choked out, tears spilling freely.

"I love you so much," she murmured against my hair.

Darian stood apart, watching silently. He understood. This was our moment.

When we pulled away, she wiped her eyes, then turned brisk once again, her composure restored. "We don't have much time. The berries are ready—and so are you. What is the latest from the Council?"

I hesitated, searching her face. She was not the stranger who had haunted my memories. But nor was she the mother I remembered.

"King Thalor is dead," I said.

Her expression did not break. Only her eyes darkened. She turned to Darian. Their gazes met. He gave a single nod.

Her reaction was neither the shock nor the grief I expected. It was acceptance. Understanding.

"This changes everything," she murmured. Then she straightened. "But we can't linger. There's more you need to know—but it has to wait."

Without another word, she began gathering the Emberberries and supplies with swift, deliberate motions. At last, she glanced back at us, her face tight with resolve.

"Come. We will go to Aquara."

With our packs full and the weight of unspoken truths heavier still, we followed her away from the North of all Norths and back toward the world waiting to unravel.

28

The Throne

The streets of Aquara were a storm.

I had expected unrest, but this was anarchy. Chaos poured from every alleyway and every courtyard. People clawed at the gates of the King's Palace, screaming, *"Where's our water?!"*

The Royal Guard's commands vanished beneath the roar of the mob. Glass shattered. Wood splintered. People screamed.

We pushed forward, boots slipping on debris-strewn cobblestones, hearts hammering against our ribs. When we arrived at the Royal Gates, the crowds were so dense that it was impossible for the guards on the other side to let us in.

The crowd pushed against the gates. Soon, the force of the mass turned into a rocking motion, like a pendulum. Unlike a pendulum, the back-and-forth swings intensified. Then…

CRACK!

The gate structure snapped from its foundation, bringing the entire steel frame to the ground. People rushed in, running over the gates that lay flat on the ground.

As we were swept by the crowds into the Palace grounds, a small body slammed into Darian and me, nearly knocking us off balance. Bright green eyes stared up at me through dirt-streaked cheeks.

"Solara! Darian! You're back!" Princess Vira gasped, clutching Darian's tunic with desperate strength. "Everything's worse. So much worse. We needed you—I didn't know if you were ever coming back."

Darian's hand steadied her, gentle in the chaos. "We're here now."

I brushed dirt from her tangled hair, warmth flickering through my exhaustion. "We missed you," I whispered.

Two Palace Guards recognised Darian and quickly ushered us further inward toward safety.

"Wait… where's my mother?" I shouted. I looked around, but it was going to be impossible to find her in the chaos of the moment.

"We need to move. Now!" Darian shouted back. "The guards will find her."

By now, a dozen more guards had surrounded us, and curious eyes were beginning to turn our way. We followed them.

I caught the familiar sharp smell of boiled herbs emanating from the half-open windows of the Palace Infirmary long before we stepped inside—but nothing could have prepared me for the chorus of moans drifting out from within.

Every cot was filled. Tables, benches, even the stone floor had been turned into makeshift beds. Faces I knew—people who had once smiled at me, argued with me, lived beside me—lay pale and fevered, blotches eating at their skin. Healers rushed past, voices a blur of clipped demands.

Fetch more poultice.

Another bandage—hurry!

Does she look steady?

And all the while, Vira clung to my side, her eyes taking in the devastation.

"The rebels," she whispered. "They poisoned Aquara's reservoirs. The bombs were just a distraction. We've had no clean water for three days." Her lips trembled. "This is the last day."

The words hollowed me out. An entire city condemned. Children, mothers, soldiers—all doomed.

"The Council hoards what's left," Vira added bitterly. "They hide in their chambers, rationing water among themselves while people die in the streets. The Guard is dragging strangers into conscription. There is no heir. We are lost."

I gripped her hand. "No. Not lost. We've found water. Enough for everyone. Darian's Guard is already on the move."

Her tears slowed. "Hey, Solara… when were you going to tell me you had a mother?"

"Vira, it's complicated…"

Before I could say more, Mother's voice cut in. "Not complicated enough to keep from you, dear."

I turned. My mother stood in the archway, pale but radiant, her eyes fierce and unyielding despite the exhaustion etched in her face. The infirmary noise fell away. For a heartbeat, it was only us.

"Mother," I breathed, stumbling into her arms. She held me as if she had been waiting her whole life for this embrace. When at last she drew back, her hand lingered on my cheek.

The door slammed open.

A maid, breathless, bowed low. "Your Highness, Prince Darian is addressing the people."

My chest tightened. *Already?*

We hurried after her, the sound of the crowd swelling with every turn through the Palace's stone corridors. You could feel the low murmur building into a storm. When we finally reached the balcony, I froze.

Below, the city was a living sea. Thousands pressed shoulder to shoulder, overflowing the streets, courtyards, even rooftops. Faces, gaunt and desperate, all tilted upward toward the Palace. Soldiers ringed the steps, High Lords hovered stiffly at the edges and Commanders stood grim and silent.

At the top of the King's Balcony, overlooking the Palace grounds, stood Darian.

Hundreds of drones made their way to every town square and around the Palace perimeter. They were already filling the air with holograms of Darian—sixty times larger and blasting his voice at deafening decibels.

He started, "Brothers and sisters of Aquara. For too long, we have hoarded what should have been shared. Water, grain, bread—we built walls while others starved. And now, those walls have crumbled. Poisoned wells have shown us the truth: greed cannot save us. Hoarding cannot save us. Only unity can."

The restless crowd stirred, murmurs swelling like a tide.

"The age of walls is over," Darian's voice cut through the noise. "No realm greater, no realm lesser. If Aetherium is to rise, we rise together—or we all fall."

The murmurs broke into a roar.

"DARIAN! DARIAN! DARIAN!"

He lifted one hand, and he waited until the roar silenced.

"Please," he said, voice steady. "Kneel for the true heir."

My breath caught. A thousand eyes swung toward us. My knees nearly buckled.

"Solara Hawkthorne," Darian declared, his voice ringing against the stone. "Your Forgotten Queen."

The Palace grounds and every square in the Realm erupted. A tidal wave shook Aetherium to its bones.

The roar of the crowd rattled the balcony windows behind me, a living thunder rolling through the Palace walls.

Was I ready for this? I turned to Mother. She did not speak. She did not need to. Her steady nod meant more than any words.

My heart should have been pounding violently. Instead, a strange calm came over me, steady and unyielding.

Fight.

It was the same force I had felt when I absorbed the venomous tendrils of Blotchbane from Darian's body only a few days ago. Only now, the force was being nourished by the energy of the crowds. I had not tasted Emberberry in months; my power was soaring.

This was my moment.

I stepped forward to the edge of the balcony and faced my people.

Every eye was on me. Every voice silenced.

I drew in a breath. "My name is Solara Hawkthorne. Some of you know me as a healer. Many of you do not know me at all. It is because the King's Council wanted me forgotten."

A ripple stirred through the crowd, whispers catching like sparks.

"But I was born in this Palace. I carry the blood of Kings—and the scars of the people. I was hidden not because I was unworthy, but because I was dangerous to those who hoarded power while our children died of thirst."

I let my gaze sweep over them—soldiers, mothers, elders, children clinging to their parents.

"You've been lied to. You've been starved. You've been left to die while others drank freely behind marble walls. But today, that ends."

I raised my voice, steady now. "We have found water. Pure water, enough to last for generations. It will flow to every realm—Terra, Haren, Ignios, Aquara. Not one drop hoarded. Not one child left to thirst."

The murmur rose, louder, a tide rising.

"From this day forward, no family will bury a child because of a law written in greed. No realm will suffer while another wastes. We will tear down the walls that divided us and rebuild Aetherium, not as four fractured realms, but as one people. One future."

The roar swelled—but I raised my hand, and the crowd quieted again.

"But hear me now," I said, my voice dropping, sharper than before. "If we are to begin again, it cannot be with vengeance in our hearts. We will not poison tomorrow with the hatreds of yesterday. Yes, those in power wronged us. Yes, they stole from us. But if we answer with bitterness alone, we will only build new walls in place of the old."

I let the silence stretch, then turned toward the balconies where the Council stood in their silks and jewels.

"To the Council," I said, my words cutting through the air like steel, "I offer forgiveness—but not power. Your rule ends today. Effective immediately, you will retire. You will no longer sit in chambers of politics or hold command in the military. You will live as citizens among the people you once sought to control. That is your chance at redemption: to embrace a fairer world, not to forge it. You had your chance. You squandered it."

Gasps rippled through the crowd. Councilors shifted uneasily, but none dared speak.

"Know this," I continued, my voice unwavering. "Any breach of this—any attempt to seize power again—will be met with severe punishment. Because Aetherium cannot, will not, fall back into your hands."

The crowd roared, the sound rolling like a wave against the Palace walls.

A silence fell, deep and heavy.

"I forgive them," I said simply. "Not because they deserve it, but because we deserve peace. Because forgiveness is the only key that can unlock our future. And I ask you to forgive too. Not to forget. Never forget. But to choose a different road."

I lifted my fist high. As I scanned the crowd, my gaze caught on a lone figure in a black hooded cloak. She was raising her fist to meet mine. As her hood fell back and her trademark silver braids emerged, her identity was unmistakable. Our eyes locked, and in the swell of noise Rhea and I shared a quiet smile.

"The age of hoarding is over. The age of cruelty is over. Today, we turn the page. Today, we write the beginning of a new story. Together."

The crowd erupted. A thundering sound rumbled across the realms, like the earth itself breaking open.

"SOLARA! SOLARA! SOLARA!"

Darian's hand came to rest on my shoulder—steady, relieved. My mother's eyes gleamed with pride.

For the first time, I felt it settle deep in my bones.

I was not forgotten.

I was not powerless.

I was their Queen.

About The Author

Zoe Karibian is a 17-year-old writer living in London.

As a journalist and editor, her work has been recognized by the National Scholastic Press Association and the Columbia Scholastic Press Association—including the title of Freshman Journalist of the Year 2023.

Outside of journalism, Zoe enjoys pottery, breaking down films and finding creative ways to engage young writers as part of her school's Creative Writing Club.

Her stories often reflect themes of heritage, survival and resilience.